# Pa'u Hana

### By:
### Steve Akley

PUBLISHED BY S.A.P. ENTERTAINMENT

# Written by:
# Steve Akley

Printed in the United States of America

Published by S.A.P. Entertainment © 2015

ISBN: 978-0-9906060-4-8

**Dedicated to my friends and fans in Hawai'i:**
Many alohas and a big mahalo nui loa for
being so supportive of my writing efforts!

Kaua'i

Ni'ihau

O'ahu

Moloka'i

Maui

Lāna'i

Kaho'olawe

Hawai'i
"The Big Island"

# Pa'u Hana

Noun

*(Pow-Ha-Nah)*

*A uniquely Hawaiian phrase. Translated directly, it literally means "after work." Typically, it is utilized to denote the time after work has been completed when an individual can relax and have fun with friends.*

# Table of Contents

# Pa'u Hana

## –: KAUA'I :–

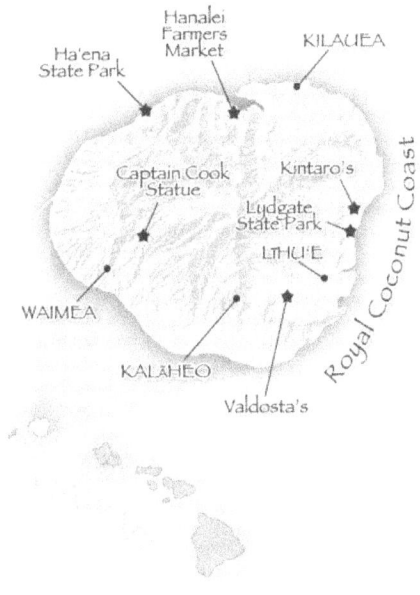

**8:37 a.m.**
**Līhu'e Civic Center**
**Monthly "First Thursday" Meeting**
**Highway Department/Animal Control/Parks**
**& Recreation**
**Līhu'e, Kaua'i, Hawai'i**

At the front of the conference room, Sam Māhoe, Director of Mobile Civil Services for the Island of Kaua'i, is addressing 44 of his team members along with 3 representatives from the police department for his monthly meeting. The state government offices without offices on Kaua'i which report to Sam are Animal Control, the Highway Department and Parks and Recreation. Other than Animal Control, which is just two individuals who work independently based on need, Sam's groups work in crews out in the field on assigned crews and jobs.

The idea for a first Thursday of the month meeting was born out of necessity. The road crews from the Highway Department weren't working together. Neither were the Parks and Recreation teams. This lack of communication led to a multitude of issues. Like the time the Parks team showed up to clean-up the foliage at the entrance to Koke'e State Park the same time one of the road crews was tearing out the road at the entrance. By the time the road crew's work was completed, all of the plants the Parks team shipped into Koke'e had died.

Under Sam's leadership, all crews have an understanding of the other teams' projects and where each team will be working. Representatives from the police department are invited through an agreement between Sam Māhoe and Chief Aukai of the Kaua'i Police Department. The two organizations have found it best if both units are fully aware and informed of the details of upcoming Civil Services projects.

Work has not only been smoother, but simply knowing the other teams from the monthly meetings has led to a much more harmonious relationship between all entities involved. Right now, though, two team members at the back of the room are ignoring Sam Māhoe as he speaks to Road Crew D regarding road repairs in Waimea near the Captain Cook statue.

Danny Bandera and Rex Palakiko are the newest member of the Kaua'i Parks and Recreation team. They were hired six months ago as the fourth two-person crew. Not only did their hiring mean an increase from three to four teams, Bandera and Palakiko work Wednesday to Sunday meaning Kaua'i now has teams working seven days a week. Another feather in the cap of Sam Māhoe.

Danny Bandera, 45, was a twenty-year veteran of the St. Louis County Parks Department in Missouri. He had been a rising star for S.L.C.P.D., but elected to leave his position when he found out his director had been having an affair with his wife. With no children, he decided a new job and a divorce meant it might be a good time to simply start over. After the divorce was finalized, he sold or gave away almost everything he owned, removed himself from all social media and moved to Kaua'i. Sight unseen. He didn't know anyone there. He had never visited. He certainly had heard it was beautiful and peaceful, but it was literally all he knew.

Having lived here for almost six months now, he has found the entire island of Kaua'i to have a really small town feel, which, while quiet, wasn't totally desolate, either. It seems to be the perfect paradise for someone wanting to get away from everything back in his hometown of St. Louis.

Not having a real plan when he arrived, he literally slept on the beach his first night. At first, he thought he might try his hand at being an artist. A lifelong hobby painter, he was thinking of simply painting landscapes and selling them to tourists. Just like you hear about on the streets of France.

There was certainly a tourist trade he could market his craft to and the appeal of not having a boss was calling to him. The more he thought about it, though, the less appealing it sounded. He would need to crank out paintings like a factory to produce enough to sell. Of course, the actual creation of the paintings only represented the starting point of his work. He would then need to actually market and sell them. It kind of started sounding like a job, minus the benefits and steady income.

Lucky for Danny, Sam Māhoe happened to be putting together a fourth two-person team on his Parks Department crew when Danny started looking for a real job. His work history landed him an interview, and Sam was impressed with his knowledge. He knew he wouldn't need to spend a lot of time looking over Danny's shoulder with his experience. This was especially appealing to Sam who was dealing with managing a quickly growing staff out in the field.

One thing Danny knew he didn't want any longer was to go into management. He had been ascending the organization at the St. Louis County Parks Department, but now he wanted to be a part of a team, not lead it. The responsibilities of managing people wasn't anything which appealed to him any longer. Danny wanted to simply do his job in the beautiful Kaua'i outdoors and then go home and enjoy more of the beauty of the island.

Rex Palakiko, 27, is a native Hawaiian born and raised on the island of Kaua'i. The former professional bodyboarder has a completely different view of Kaua'i than his counterpart Danny Bandera. Though he loves his native Kaua'i, and it will always be his home, he simply couldn't help but feel the limitations of life on a small island. He felt limited and isolated at the same time.

Still, there wasn't an imminent feeling he would be leaving anytime soon. As a Native Hawaiian from Kaua'i, there is pull which only someone in his same situation can understand. There is this unforeseen force, like gravity, which tethers you to your home base.

It all goes back to Hawaiian culture where everything surrounds the "ohana," or family. Straying from your home means a departure from your family, which in-turn crumbles the ever-important family unit. Loss of family means traditions disappear and over time, Hawaiian culture itself would likely be lost.

You would think this feeling of not leaving your family on your native island would be reinforced by demands from family elders and non-stop conversations about not leaving home. That's simply not the case. In reality, it never spoken about. In fact, if Rex decided he wanted to leave, his family would be very supportive. If he walked into his parents' house tomorrow and stated he was moving to Dallas, it wouldn't be surprising for them to celebrate his announcement and maybe even present him a pair of cowboy boots at a going away gathering of family. What Rex would have to deal with would be something much more deep-rooted. A feeling in his heart. Is moving the right thing?

His family, while not expressing it outwardly, would also likely be experiencing deep-rooted angst if he left. How are the traditions of family going to be carried on by Rex and a family he starts when he's living in Texas?

Again, these are unspoken issues, but they are there, and they are always weighing on you if you are a Native Hawaiian. Rex's job with the Parks and Recreation Department is a direct result of this unforeseen force. While not as popular as surfing, there is a small and loyal group of fans for this alternative sport of bodyboarding and Rex had found a great deal of success in this counterculture. While there is a limited amount of time a person has in any athletic endeavor, Rex was still several years from his thirtieth birthday and probably had ten more years of competing ahead of him.

His career was successful, too. He had picked up sponsors and was the number one ranked bodyboarder in the world, having collected multiple cash prizes for his efforts.

He was at an event in O'ahu when he got a call his grandfather, who had been ill, took a turn for the worse and wanted to see him. When Rex arrived at his bedside, he was taken by surprise when his grandfather told him he was dying and as his final wish he wanted Rex to take a more conventional path to his career.

There is that "gravitational pull."

What could he do? He idolized his grandfather, the patriarch of the Palakiko family. He agreed on the spot to try to find a job in Kaua'i and see where it took him.

True to his word, after his grandfather's passing, he landed a job with Sam Māhoe working with Danny Bandera. Despite the nearly twenty year age difference and very diverse backgrounds, the two hit it off immediately and became good friends and key members of Māhoe's team.

You wouldn't think the duo of Bandera and Palakiko was known for their professionalism if you were watching them right now, though. While Māhoe outlined some road work he needed from Road Crew #3 in Waimea near the Captain Cook statue, Bandera and Palakiko were at the back of the room talking quietly. Danny was peeling back a bandage he had on his right inner forearm covering five colorful Grateful Dead dancing bears which would gyrate like hula dancers when he flexed his forearm.

This was Danny's seventh Grateful Dead-themed tattoo. He had the dancing terrapins on his left inner forearm and the dancing top-hatted cane-toting Uncle Sam skeletons on his belly. His chest featured an oversized Grateful Dead logo of the red, white and blue skull with the lightning bolt through it. His right bicep had the skeleton with the mandolin and his left bicep had the skull with roses. His inner lower lip had the word "deadhead" tattooed on it. His masterpiece was his full back tattoo which had a concert scene featuring six members.

As Danny brought his chorus line of dancing Grateful Dead bears to life, others began to notice and started snickering along with Palakiko. Just then, Sam Māhoe took note. "Bandera, what are you doing?" he sternly inquired.

"I'm airing out my new tattoo. You gotta let it breathe, sir," replied Bandera.

"That's not another Grateful Dead tattoo, is it? You're clinging on to a group which has been broken up for 20 years," complained Māhoe.

"Not true, sir," retorted Bandera. "They played shows this past summer in Santa Clara and Chicago. This was a big deal. Not sure how you missed that news. They sold out these shows in like…"

"Bandera!" interjected Māhoe, "We don't care about this. We're here to talk about the plan for the upcoming month. I've got you and Palakiko completing the Lydgate State Park cleanup today. You two take one of the dump trucks over there after the meeting and pick up all the trash bags the volunteers have filled up on the beach. Also, do a sweep of the entire area and see if there is anything else which needs to be removed. This was a tremendous effort from our crews and the local community. We're going to do some press releases about the cleaned up park, and I want to make sure this thing looks its best."

Māhoe continued, "Tomorrow, I want the two of you at the Līhu'e Courthouse. The governor was there last month and commented on how bad it looked. We're going to remove all of the existing foliage and rework it with some fresh plants. The rest of the month I'm going to need you two at Ha'ena State Park. We're going to use the model of our work at Lydgate with Ha'ena as well. Complete beach clean-up, replanting of foliage and a refreshing of the facilities. One other thing, I know you guys are off Monday and Tuesday typically, but I need you two to fly to Honolulu on Monday for a meeting with the team there. They have been successful in getting their parks cleaned up and want to show you some of their ideas. We'll work out a comp day later for working on your day off. Get with Diane to arrange your travel to O'ahu. All of this works out perfectly since you can gather up and start on the trash clean-up on Sunday. You can put together a plan to get the entire area cleaned. I will have some volunteers lined up to assist you in really getting down to making Ha'ena look good, and I'll have a construction crew there on Wednesday to get the bathroom renovations going."

When the meeting ended, just as Sam Māhoe had instructed, Danny Bandera and Rex Palakiko jumped into a Kaua'i County dump truck and headed towards Lydgate State Park in nearby Kapa'a.

Before getting to their job site, Rex and Danny stopped at Chicken in a Barrel BBQ for lunch. It's always kind of odd dining on barbecued chicken with feral roosters and chickens running around this outdoor dining establishment. You start to wonder where they are getting their supplies. Once you take your first bite, though, you really don't care.

That was some tasty barbecued bird!

After their meal, they pulled into Lydgate State Park. The Lydgate cleanup had been a large undertaking. A rock wall was built which created a lagoon keeping larger ocean fish out but allowing smaller fish in for some great snorkeling. The picnic tables had been replaced. The bathroom facilities upgraded; a playground was added for the kiddies. The last order of business was to remove the hundreds (and hundreds) of bags of trash which had been gathered up by county workers and volunteers.

This seemingly endless number of bags faced Rex and Danny as they arrived. Rather than getting down about the work ahead of them, they simply did what they always did, jumped in and started working while talking about the mundane topics of everyday life to pass the time away.

**Rex:** Hey Danny, I overheard Joe Pimentel call Gene Randle a trouser pilot at work today. Joe said he heard some bit on Letterman once. Letterman said he had his legal team vet out the worst thing you could call someone without damaging their reputation to the point of them having legal recourse. Apparently, that phrase is trouser pilot.

**Danny:** Trouser pilot? I like it. It's equally offensive to either male or female, and the fact it's been vetted out by legal is comforting. I'm going to use it. I'm thinking it may even make the heavy rotation.

**Rex:** What's the worst thing you ever called a co-worker? I mean there are certain phrases, which rightfully so, would get you fired immediately. I'm not talking sexual harassment, racial stuff, that sort of thing. I'm saying the absolute worst thing you ever called someone without getting fired.

**Danny:** I actual know the answer to this one. Back when I worked in St. Louis, we would have to go into the office. This one woman who worked there was really annoying. The know-it-all type. The funny thing was, this "know-it-all" lived in Fenton.

**Rex:** Fenton?

**Danny:** Yeah, that doesn't mean anything to you, but Fenton is this small town in the suburbs of St. Louis. It straddles the line between St. Louis County and Jefferson County. Jefferson County butts up against St. Louis and is the start of the wilderness in Missouri. Missouri is a largely rural state. You have St. Louis on the east side, Kansas City on the west side and not a lot in between. It's like once you cross the line into Jefferson County out of St. Louis County the laws and decorum of city living quickly disappear. You've got cars parked in front yards, people riding horses, cornfields, banjos.

**Rex:** Banjos?

**Danny:** All right. I can't actually back up the banjos comment, but you're getting the idea. A completely different world opened up via the invisible gateway of a county line. So the town of Fenton is actually situated half in Jefferson County and half in St. Louis County. If you aren't from the area, it's just a town. If you live in St. Louis, this is the vortex of evil. You don't want to be from Fenton. So this Miss Know-It-All actually not only lives in Fenton, she was born there, and every experience she shares goes back to Fenton. She wants to share everything about her life, but everything she talks about is Fenton. If your only experiences in life are limited to the cornpone world of Fenton, in reality, you don't have a lot to share... unless of course you are the know-it-all/share-it-all type... which, as I've already made clear, she certainly was.

So this story starts out simple enough. Miss Know-It-All had just told me how she normally eats only at Fenton restaurants. Actually, most of her meals are at this gas station by her house, but that's a different story. Anyway, she says she had heard good things about Dewey's Pizza in Kirkwood, which is a much nicer suburban community like 5 miles away.

She hated it. She had a whole list of reasons but filtering through her blather, I could tell the number one thing it had working against it was the fact it wasn't domiciled in Fenton. By chance, just after she was telling me she didn't like it, another co-worker, who felt the same way about this woman as I did, was telling me how he had recently eaten at Dewey's Pizza for the first time. He was detailing how much he liked it. Even though I had eaten Dewey's Pizza before, and really like it, I couldn't help but give him a dig by telling him Miss Know-It-All had just blasted it.

Well, this guy goes off. The first thing out of his mouth was, "Let me tell you, that Fenton-bred clown eats taquitos off a roller five nights a week, she has no idea what good food is."

Man, I just lost it. "Fenton-bred clown." It killed me. It just perfectly summed up this woman. I had tears in my eyes I was laughing so hard.

**Rex:** So you called her a Fenton-bred clown?

**Danny:** I wish. It's worse than that. It did stick with me, and I thought I would use it at some point. Sure enough, a few weeks later, I told her she should go to this barbecue festival they were having in downtown St. Louis. She informed me she only goes to festivals and parades in Fenton. Knowing the excitement of Fenton Days Parades are about as thrilling as Sunday dinner at Grandma's, it was time to break out the line so I dropped it on her, only my mouth wasn't in sync with my brain and I instead stated, "Listen you Fenton-bred cow…"

Soon as it got out, my brain caught up. It was a horrible thing to say, obviously, but still, I couldn't properly apologize because every time the line "Fenton-bred cow" went through my head, I started uncontrollably laughing. I'm trying to say it was our other co-workers line, and it should be Fenton-bred clown… but I can't properly apologize because I'm laughing like a hyena. Body shaking… more laughter. Even tears.

I was legitimately sorry, mind you. I didn't want to call her that, but the more I tried to think about it, the worse it got.

**Rex:** Was she fat?

**Danny:** Well… I mean she was from Fenton. There's only so much you can do. What about you? Did you ever say something to a co-worker which was over the line?

**Rex:** Well, considering this is my first real job, I don't have a story like yours. I once had an incident with my Anakē Marlene.

**Danny:** Anakē?

**Rex:** My aunt. She always sang this song, "Ya ta ta-ta, ya ta ta-ta, the treasures of summer."

**Danny:** Okay.

**Rex:** No, I mean consistently, on a loop, ya ta ta-ta, ya ta ta-ta, the treasures of summer. No other words, just two ya ta ta-tas and the line the treasures of summer. I don't think there were any other words. I'm not even sure it's a real song.

**Danny:** Was this like a tic? She just did it without knowing?

**Rex:** I think it was a nervous habit just to kind of fill in the open gaps of no conversation. Whenever the family got together, Anakē Marlene always did the dishes. I don't know. It was just kind of her thing. Of course, during dish time, there is plenty of dead air, and Anakē Marlene keeps singing it over and over and over…

Ya ta ta-ta, ya ta ta-ta, the treasures of summer.

There would be a short pause, and then:

Ya ta ta-ta, ya ta ta-ta, the treasures of summer.

You always hear about prisoners of war and non-harmful torture tactics. They get worn down by some sort of repetitive activity. Well, I can assure you, this phenomena is real because I finally snapped. She starts back up "Ya ta ta-ta, ya ta…" and I just blurted out, "Anakē Marlene, it's Thanksgiving, there are no treasures of summer right now."

**Danny:** Did she quit singing?

**Rex:** Well, I don't actually know what happened in terms of the immediate aftermath. I was like ten at the time. My mom dove across a table as soon as I said it. She grabbed me by the shirt collar, and I was immediately ushered out of the kitchen and into my room the rest of the night. The next ohana time, the treasures of summer serenade returned, but I didn't dare say a word. I continued to hear that song every time I saw her for the rest of her life. Unfortunately, she passed away just a few years later. You know what's weird?

**Danny:** What?

**Rex:** I hated that song. I dreaded the thought that it would be sung the whole time she was at the house. I couldn't stand when she was actually singing it. Now, I really wish I could her sing it one more time. Sometimes I find myself singing that little ditty.

**Danny:** You want a hug or something?

**Rex:** Get out of here, man. Hey, how are we doing here? Are we making any progress?

As Rex and Danny surveyed the area, the seemingly endless supply wasn't showing any signs of disappearing any time soon. As they continued on, each with bags of trash in both hands, Rex stopped them.

**Rex:** Hold on Danny, I have to tie my shoe.

**Danny:** What? Your shoes are tied.

**Rex:** No, it's the left one.

**Danny:** Rex, it's tied. The left one is tied, the right one is tied. What are you doing?

As Rex bent down to tie his left shoe, he continued, "It is still tied, but it's a little loose. It's not as tight as the right one. They have to be equal, otherwise it doesn't feel right, and I have trouble walking.

**Danny:** Trouble walking?

**Rex:** Yes, it's like my shoe is going to fall off.

**Danny:** It's tied.

**Rex:** I don't know. It's loose. It's not right. Anyway, it's tied now.

**Danny:** So let's go.

**Rex:** Wait, I have to tie my right shoe now.

**Danny:** You said it was the left shoe.

**Rex:** It was. Over time, your shoes loosen up. Most of the time we don't even notice it because we wear the shoes, take them off in an hour or two and then retie them the next time we wear them, thereby reestablishing that base of a tightly-tied shoelace.

**Danny:** Yeah, fine. Your left shoe was the loose one.

**Rex:** I know. Perhaps I wasn't perfect in tying it this morning. Maybe I hit something which unbound it slightly. I don't know. Anyway, once I just retied it, establishing a new tight base, I was able to feel the difference between a now freshly tied, and reestablished base on my left, versus my right foot which was going through the normal untying process I just outlined to you which occurs naturally throughout the day. I had to remedy the situation with a preventative shoe re-tie to avoid thinking about every step on that right shoe.

**Danny:** What if I stopped what I was doing right now and untied your left shoe?

**Rex:** I would tie it.

**Danny:** What about the right one?

**Rex:** It's tied.

**Danny:** Yes, but the left would have just gotten untied. Don't we need to reestablish our base?

**Rex:** No. I told you the loosening of the base occurs during your normal routine. I just tied the right. It's still got the established firm base. Now if you'd try to untie my left shoe, yes, there could perhaps be a little wear and tear on the base from my trying to kick you in the head, but I'm thinking it's still fine. Speaking of loosening, your bandage is starting to come off of your new tattoo. I don't think you should have taken it off during the meeting. Bandages give you one good sticking. Peel it back one time, it's over.

**Danny:** It's fine. I can just take the bandage off now.

**Rex:** What is your fascination with the Grateful Dead anyway?

**Danny:** I followed them. For two years after high school, I rode around everywhere the Dead went in my 1974 AMC Gremlin.

**Rex:** I thought people used those old VW busses to follow the Dead.

**Danny:** You can. In fact, many do. You could also use whatever car you wanted. It's not about the cars, the clothes, the lifestyle with the Dead. It was about the music.

**Rex:** I thought it was about community? A group of outcasts from society, bound by their love of music, in particular the music of the Grateful Dead, who created their own pseudo-society. That's why they had the big set-ups around the venues. Cars parked with people camping in them. People partying. Followers selling crafts and toasted cheese sandwiches. The Dead is all about a sense of community and an alternative society, my friend. The music is a bit player. Your stars are the sense of community, an alternate universe, drugs and characters. The Dead were like caricatures of musicians these people loved like a child loves his or her teddy bear.

**Danny:** Not true. Well, not true for me and plenty of others. Today, they don't even need musicians. They could use holographic images playing the same sets at a different venue each night. That's what people want these days. It cracks me up we now actually have holograms entertaining people. Wow, Tupac had a great show the other night!

They just want this perfect sound of something being played the exact same way in the exact same order each night. They could blindfold you, take you to a show in Philadelphia and then do the same thing in Boston the next night and ask you to compare and contrast the two performances. Your response would have to be they are exactly the same!

**Rex:** So, what are you saying? You don't like great music?

**Danny:** Why is exactly the same every night considered great music?

**Rex:** Consistency.

**Danny:** Consistency? Consistency blows! That's why there is no following with today's musicians. Their performances are exactly the same. Why would I see a show in St. Louis then drive to Kansas City to see the exact same show. I've already seen it.

**Rex:** I thought you liked the music. If it's the music, don't you want to see it again?

**Danny:** No! I could download the song and hear that version a hundred times a day. What I loved about the Dead was the fact each night was an event, seemingly being developed right before your eyes live on the stage. These guys weren't pumping out the exact same song they had played 1,000 times before, they were creating art right on the stage. Let me tell you, I have hundreds of their concerts on tape. I probably have 50 different versions of songs you would know. I'm not talking archaic stuff, I'm talking about if you have any interest in the Grateful Dead you know these songs. Like, say the song *Truckin'*. Each version has different nuances, intros, riffs that make it unique. It becomes the '82 version of *Truckin'* from Dallas, that type of thing. You haven't experienced that song, unless you have happened to hear a tape of the night it was played. See, it's about the music.

**Rex:** So if Katy Perry changed up her songs each night, you'd like her?

**Danny:** Katy Perry is the complete opposite of being about the music. I don't know anything about Katy Perry other than what you see on the news or in interviews. When I see her talking, she's sharing about the number of outfit changes fans will see. Outfit changes! Are you kidding me? Who cares? No, Katy Perry will play her idiotic songs for a base of young teenagers who will adore her until they realize her music is complete trash and then her career will be seemingly over until those teenagers grow up, get married, have kids of their own and yearn for their youth and then we'll see a ballooned up version of Katy Perry singing that same nonsense as she changes into very flowing outfits as opposed to the tight stuff she wears today.

**Rex:** Whoa, you are angry about this stuff.

**Danny:** Because I love music and nobody plays music anymore. Well, almost no one. Tell me Rex, who do you like?

**Rex:** Well, besides Katy Perry, of course?

**Danny:** Of course.

**Rex:** I would have to go with Chumbawumba.

**Danny:** What?

**Rex:** You know, Chumbawumba? They sing that song *Tubthumping*. It goes (singing), "*I get knocked down and I get up again.*"

**Danny:** Okay, okay. Yes, I know it. Why would you like them?

**Rex:** Oh man, I love that song *Tubthumping*. It's an anthem, man.

**Danny:** What?

**Rex:** Oh yeah, it calls to me. It's an ode to drinking. It's got that chant, a trumpet solo and what about the middle? They break into a traditional version of

*Danny Boy.* Talk about melding the new and the old. It gives me goosebumps just talking about it.

**Danny:** Cha-what?ba?

**Rex:** Chumbawamba.

**Danny:** That's your favorite group?

**Rex:** Yes.

**Danny:** Of all-time?

**Rex:** From the beginning of time, or my birth, however you are setting this up; Chumbawamba is the band for me. Man, those guys really can play a mean *Tubthumping.* (singing) *I get knocked down, and I get up again!*

**Danny:** What's your second favorite Chumbawamba song?

**Rex:** (thinking for a moment) I would have to say that traditional version of *Danny Boy* ensconced in the middle of *Tubthumping*.

**Danny:** Chumbawamba is a novelty act. A one hit wonder, who, if they are even still together, is probably playing county fairs and smoke-filled casinos. Here's a real band… (Danny rips off his shirt exposing a tattoo covering his back of the Grateful Dead playing a concert).

**Rex:** Whoa. What do you have going on there?

**Danny:** Fillmore East. That's the historic Grateful Dead concert from February 13, 1970. That guy you see standing next to Jerry Garcia is Duane Allman. The Duane Allman of the Allman Brothers. It's considered one of the greatest live events of all-time. Two of the greatest jam bands jamming together like nothing the world has ever seen before or since.

**Rex:** So you memorialize the event in ink on your back?

**Danny:** Well, there's more to it than that. My parents had tickets to the concert.

**Rex:** Oh, so they saw it.

**Danny:** Actually, no.

**Rex:** What? So it's a tragedy? They forgot about it? Stuck in traffic? Drug haze? Got ahold of bad grilled cheese sandwich?

**Danny:** No to all of the above. They drove all the way up there from St. Louis. They knew it was going to be an epic event. Clearly they had no idea about the magnitude it was going to be, but as fans of the Grateful Dead, Fillmore East was going to be big. They park and get ready to go in. My mom turns to my dad and says, "Larry, it's time. I'm going to have this kid."

**Rex:** Your mom was pregnant?

**Danny:** Yep. Probably not the smartest thing to do, but they really wanted to see that show. They had asked her doctor, he said it should be fine so they drove all the way to the show. After realizing this was happening right now, my dad took my mom to the hospital. Even though I am sure some Deadhead would have probably stepped up and helped with the delivery my parents were smart enough to take me to the hospital. They ended up not having much time to spare as I was born shortly after they arrived.

**Rex:** Probably right about the time Duane Allman took the stage!

**Danny:** Exactly. February 13, 1970. Man, my dad whined about that the rest of his life. The best part about the whole story was the fact my dad talked about it so much I became a Dead fan.

**Rex:** Okay. Now the tattoos make sense. Well, as much sense as a 40-something year old man getting tattoos of a defunct band can make sense.

**Danny:** Not defunct. Not actively playing right now, but not defunct. They had those shows in Santa Clara and Chicago this past summer, and you can still catch Bob Weir or Phil Lesh working independently or collaborating together occasionally.

**Rex:** They should pair up with Chumbawumba.

**Danny:** Oh yeah. Lesh and Weir could play for 3 hours and Chumbawumba could roll out with *Tubthumping* which incorporates a shortened version of *Danny Boy* and then just play their second biggest hit, *Danny Boy,* to round out their set.

**Rex:** Sounds pretty good.

**Danny:** Hey, we are done. It looks awesome. Māhoe is going to love this. Let's drop off the dump truck and then it's pa'u hana time my friend.

**Rex:** Automatic! Let's go to Kintaro's.

**Danny:** Kintaro's it is! First round is on Rex.

One of the first places Rex introduced Danny to when they started working together was Kintaro Japanese Restaurant, or as it was simply known by the local crowd: Kintaro's.

Kintaro's is a sushi restaurant frequented by the locals and is the place to mingle on the Royal Coconut Coast. Whenever Rex and Danny are working in the area, they always drop by for a dinner and some drinks. They strolled in and were pleased to see Emily, their favorite waitress was on duty in the bar. They grabbed a small table and started talking.

**Rex:** Danny, do you think working for the Parks and Recreation Department is it for you?

**Danny:** I do. They treat you well. I like working outside and where better to work outside than Kaua'i? Māhoe is a good guy, too.

**Rex:** I see what you are saying, but there has to be something more. Is there anything else you would like to do… say they laid us off tomorrow, what would you do?

**Emily (interrupting):** Hey sweeties. What can I get you guys tonight?

**Rex:** Līhue Brewing Coconut Stout.

**Danny:** Hapa Brown Ale.

**Emily:** Sounds good, I'll get those right out.

**Rex:** So, Danny, if by some circumstance we were no longer working for Māhoe, what would you do?

**Danny:** I've got a million dollar idea. I can't share it, though.

**Rex:** Why not?

**Danny:** You don't share ideas like this. Sharing it is basically giving it away. I wouldn't just give you a million dollars. Why would I give you a million dollar idea?

**Rex:** I'd give you a million dollars if I had it.

**Danny:** No you wouldn't.

**Rex:** Sure I would.

**Danny:** Why would you give me a million dollars?

**Emily:** Coconut Stout and a Hapa Brown. Anything to eat tonight?

**Danny:** Hanalei Roll.

**Rex:** Tin Foil Special.

**Danny:** Is that Coconut Stout any good?

**Rex:** Oh yeah, you have to get one of these. It's like a toasted coconut stout. It's animals.

**Danny:** Can I try it?

**Rex:** Sure. Just order one the next round. Anyway, I want to clarify… if I had it, I don't have a million to spare by the way, but if I had an extra mil laying around, you could have it.

**Danny:** Come on.

**Rex:** I'm serious. I'm a simple guy. I don't need much beyond the basics to keep me happy. Here we are at Kintaro's, lots of talent all around, some beers on the way and some food soon. That's all great, but you know where I would have been hanging out and drinking seven months ago instead of here?

**Danny:** The beach?

**Rex:** Tourists drink at the beach, Danny. Definitely not the beach. Foodland.

**Danny:** The grocery store?

**Rex:** Yes. Just on the parking lot of Foodland. I mean everything you need is there. Alcohol. Food. A Saturday night at Foodland. It's a meat market… and I'm not talking about white smocks and paper hats.

**Danny:** Beer in a paper bag, Cheetos and parking and women who have lowered their expectations to the point they are trolling Foodland's parking lot. Sounds great.

**Rex:** My point is that I don't want to live the life of a millionaire. With all of that money, there is also a lot of stress and responsibility. I want more than this island can offer, but I'm not looking for the finer things. Just something different from time-to-time. So give me two million bucks, I've got a million for my friend Danny. I'll keep the second million for myself and just live a laid back life on the beach. So now how about telling me about that million dollar idea?

**Danny:** All right, fine. When I got here, I didn't know what I was going to do. I told you I had thought about being an artist but that didn't work out. One thing I didn't tell you about was this great idea I had been thinking about long before I got here: Cartoos.

**Rex:** What?

**Danny:** Cartoos. You know like cartoons without the "n". It's a combination of car and tattoos.

**Rex:** How does that work?

**Danny:** Well, seemingly everyone is getting tattoos today. It's a way to express yourself and show off things you really care about. I like the idea of doing the same thing for cars. You have artists painting detailed artwork on people's vehicles. It could be as simple as a butterfly or as intricate as the Fillmore East show I have on my back.

**Rex:** Actually, that's not a bad idea.

**Emily:** Tin Foil Special and a Hanalei Roll. Can I get you two anything else right now?

**Rex:** Have you started carrying chili water yet?

**Emily:** Not yet. I talked to our manager. He says there isn't enough demand.

**Rex:** Not enough demand. It's like the official condiment of Kaua'i. People aren't using it because places like this don't put it on the table anymore.

**Emily:** Sorry, Rex. Beyond the chili water, which we don't have but I'll continue to press for, is there anything else I can get you two?

**Danny:** Actually, one of those Līhue Brewing Coconut Stouts for me. Thanks.

**Rex:** I can't believe they refuse to carry chili water. I need to just start bringing my own everywhere I go. Anyway, I was saying, that's a really good idea. With your artist abilities that might really fly. I mean I see a lot of people decorating their car with those stick figure families or memorials for lost love ones. Why not broaden those horizons with tattoos. I would get my dad's police badge on the back of my Jeep.

**Danny:** Exactly. You can get whatever you want. It's as open to ideas as regular tattoos are.

**Rex:** Why didn't you do this?

**Danny:** Well, I looked into a spot. You know that oil change place in Līhu'e that shut down?

**Rex:** Yeah, sure.

**Danny:** Well, I tried to open up there. Get this, I didn't want any modifications to the building. It's two bays with garage doors on each side so you can have the cars drive in and tattoo 'em up and send them on their way. With the security deposit, first and last month's rent and signage changes the guy wanted $25,000. I didn't have $25,000. The bank laughed at the thought of loaning money to me for a business called Cartoos by the way.

**Rex:** Man, that story sucks. I know that business would work. I have a business idea.

**Danny:** Wait is a drive-in car tattoo business?

**Rex:** No. I gave you my word. That's your idea. My idea is a 4¢ Store.

**Danny:** What can you buy for four cents?

**Rex:** That hat you're wearing.

**Danny:** It's a Grateful Dead hat from their shows in Chicago this past summer. It cost $45.

**Rex:** What if I could sell it to you for less?

**Danny:** Four cents? I'll take 6,000 of them, please.

**Rex:** No, not four cents. But say $40… ish.

**Danny:** Five dollars off? Big deal.

**Rex:** Ten percent, or so, doesn't sound like a lot, but if you rack up those savings on everything you buy it starts to add up pretty quickly.

**Danny:** I don't know why am doing this, but you've got me. Here I go. I'm doing this. How can you save me this money?

**Rex:** I won't charge you sales tax.

**Danny:** Number one. You will go to jail. Number two, this hat was bought at a concert, so there is no tax and number three, see number one.

**Rex:** First of all, you know how sales tax works, right?

**Danny:** Apparently better than you. I'm not scheming on a plan to open a store where I don't charge it. I agree, it would work… for like forty-two days. Just long enough to rack up felony charges then the local and federal authorities would catch on, and you'd go away for quite a while.

**Rex:** Apparently, you have no clue. You said your hat didn't have sales tax. You know they have the tax figured in on these flat rate purchases at places like concerts, right? Someone is paying the tax on the hats, shirts and posters they are selling.

**Danny:** Okay. I agree with you there.

**Rex:** My way around the tax code is to beat them at their own game. Everything in my store sells for 4¢, hence the name, the 4¢ Store.

**Danny:** You were just going to ding me $40 for my hat.

**Rex:** No I wasn't. I was going to charge you (taking out his phone for a calculator)… 1,000 four cent transactions.

**Danny:** What does that mean?

**Rex:** Rather than ring you in for $40, I'd ring it up as 1,000 4¢ transactions.

**Danny:** Why 4¢?

**Rex:** If you buy something for 4¢ or less, there is no tax.

**Danny:** Seriously, what are you talking about?

**Rex:** When I was a kid, I used to go to Longs Drugs in Līhu'e. They still had penny candy. If you had a quarter, you could buy 23 pieces and it would cost 25 cents with tax. If you bought them four pieces at a time instead of all 25 at once: four pieces, four pieces, four pieces, four pieces, four pieces, one piece, you got 25 pieces of candy for the exact same amount of money.

**Danny:** They allowed you to do that?

**Rex:** If you got the right checker. What do they care? If the mean checker was on duty, you just buy four and eat it and then go in and buy four more. I was a kid, what did I have better to do than to stretch my candy budget?

**Danny:** Why is that? Why is there no tax on four pieces?

**Rex:** Sales tax is actually brackets. They don't charge tax on 1, 2, 3 or 4 cents because I guess that would be excessive. Buy one piece of penny candy and pay one cent in tax you are taxing at 100%.

**Danny:** Brah, they have to have thought of this scam before. There is probably some little used provision in the tax code just for this 4¢ Store idea of yours. Plus, what are you going to do, ring the register 1,000 times. I sure would hate to be in the express lane behind you with your one hat you are ringing up 1,000 times. It's like success, say a cart filled with $40/4¢ hats. Um, I'd like to buy 40 of these hats. Oh no, we are shut down for the rest of the day for this $360 transaction.

**Rex:** It wouldn't work like that. I'd have some tech guy develop an app that created the 1,000 transactions and chunked it out to your card in 1,000 batches. This will work.

**Danny:** The only thing positive which may happen for you out of this idea is you might land a commissary job in jail since you would then have retail experience. That has to be at the top of the food chain in terms of prison jobs. Way better than working the cafeteria, cleaning the toilets or stamping out license plates. Hey, there's Emily. You want one more before we go?

**Rex:** Sure.

**Danny:** Emily, two more Coconut Stouts. Okay, you have to have a better idea than a white collar crime, right?

**Rex:** Well, I do have one other idea. I want to develop a show called Nut Shots?

**Danny:** Is this a nightmare I'm in here? Porn, really?

**Rex:** No, not that. Jeez. My idea is a video show where they only show just the nut shots. Thirty minutes of videos of people getting slammed right in the nuts. Here's a toddler trying to play Wiffle ball, dad gets strike one to the 'nads. Feeding the goats at the zoo, Willie the Portuguese Long Hair rams a guy right in the tackle box. Guy trying to impress his buddies with a skate boarding trick in a Foodland parking lot hits the curb and lands his sweetbreads on a fire hydrant. Guy dressed as Santa gets his jingle bells jangled.

**Danny:** Okay, I get it. Why aren't there any other types of videos?

**Emily:** Two Coconut Stouts.

**Rex:** Because nobody wants them. We watch the kitty cat videos and the grandma dancing videos only so we can see people getting hit in the scrote. With each shot of a baby falling asleep while eating dinner, secretly, each viewer is thinking I sure hope somebody takes one to the spunk bunkers in the next video.

**Danny:** So you are running the show, one nut shot after the next. Who wins?

**Rex:** The viewer. There doesn't have to be some jagaloon contest with Nut Shots. The audience wins with the joy they get from watching nothing but tater shaker videos.

**Danny:** Who calls them tater shakers?

**Rex:** Hey, we have to work within the guidelines of the censors. We're already pushing it with the Nut Shots name. We have to get creative with our on-air explanations.

**Danny:** We have a long day tomorrow at the courthouse. Are you ready to get out of here?

**Rex:** Yes sir. Let's roll.

As Rex and Danny stand up they realize how long they have been at Kintaro's as they see the darkness on the parking lot. As they walk across the bar toward the door, *The Walker* by Fitz and the Tantrums is playing in the background. As the door swings open for them to leave, lead singer Michael "Fitz" Fitzpatrick, finished the first verse and the whistle solo kicks in before the chorus, 'Whhh, whhh, whhh, whhh…'

As they step outside, Danny picks it up where Fitz and the Tantrums left off, "Whhh, whhh, whhh…" He barely gets started whistling when a hand slaps across his face snapping his head around, sending his glasses and $45 Grateful Dead hat flying.

**Danny:** Are you crazy, what's wrong with you?

**Rex:** Are you crazy? Clearly you are the crazy one here. You can't whistle outside after dark?

**Danny:** What?

**Rex:** If you whistle after dark you are calling the ghosts.

**Danny:** Is this one of those Native Hawaiian things?

**Rex:** No, it's a local thing. My Tutu Marie used to always say that.

**Danny:** I'm not local!

**Rex:** Yeah, I'm sure the ghosts will check your driver's license and birth certificate to see if you are a local.

**Danny:** Brah, that really hurt.

**Rex:** Not as bad as if those ghosts would have got to you first. I'll see you in Līhu'e tomorrow.

**Danny (rubbing his cheek):** All right. My face stings.

**Rex:** Had to be done.

The next morning, they reported directly to the Līhu'e Courthouse. The foliage they were to plant was already there waiting along with a tube containing the work order from Sam Māhoe.

**Rex:** Wow, there's a little bruising on your face.

**Danny:** Yeah, when I got home you could actually see where the outline of your hand struck my face. Not cool.

**Rex:** Did you learn a lesson? It's all good if you learned something.

**Danny:** Rex is a tool? Anyway, here is what we have on tap today. Remove all dead plants from the front entrance, along the road and down the side of the parking lot. Māhoe wants Hawaiian Wedding

Flowers along the road, an Alahee hedge planted down the side of the parking lot and Native White Hibiscus to fill in the front.

**Rex:** It said Native White Hibiscus?

**Danny:** Actually it said Koki-o-key-oak-eo?

**Rex:** Okay. You had me wondering. Māhoe always uses the traditional names in his work orders. It's Koki'o Ke'okeo. You really have to work on your native pronunciations. It's embarrassing.

**Danny:** I'm trying.

**Rex:** Throaty. It's all in the throat. Not so drawn out, either. Let it flow.

They jump in by taking their new plants off of the trailer. They then begin removing the dead foliage and piling it back on the trailer. It seems like back-breaking work at first, but soon they are talking and the time starts going by quickly.

**Danny:** I have to say, I struggle with the sun. I don't want to get burnt so I wear this floppy hat. The problem is the hat makes my neck go numb.

**Rex:** Your neck goes numb?

**Danny:** Yeah. Like a dead carp is holding up my head. I just can't figure out which is the lesser of the two evils: a numb neck or the sun exposure.

**Rex:** I think you are connecting some unrelated things here.

**Danny:** What do you mean?

**Rex:** Well, a hat has nothing to do with your neck going numb.

**Danny:** Yeah, it's tough to draw that conclusion. I don't wear a hat, my neck is fine. I have the hat on, my neck is numb.

**Rex:** I'm also thinking the hat causes more issues than just a numb neck. How about a numb skull? Did you ever stop and think it's the work you are doing while you are wearing the floppy hat causing your issues rather than a 7 ounce piece of cloth perched atop your bulbous cranium?

**Danny:** I'm telling you, it's the hat!

**Rex:** Does your Grateful Dead hat cause this same problem?

**Danny:** Don't you ever, I mean ever, take a shot at my Grateful Dead hat. Of course it doesn't hurt my neck. It's a cherished piece of history more than it is a hat, by the way.

**Rex:** Well, they probably weigh the same. Why would one cause this horrific medical issue and the other nothing at all? Other than the fact one has a Grateful Dead logo, of course.

**Danny:** Maybe you're right. I don't know. I just don't like the numb neck. I'm taking the hat off.

**Rex:** I got to thinking about our conversation last night.

**Danny:** About the fact you called nuts tater shakers?

**Rex:** What? Of all the stuff we talked about last night, you assume I'm trying to jump back in on the tater shakers comment?

**Danny:** It just seems like that was something still hanging out there.

**Rex:** No, you opened up my eyes to how ridiculous the 4¢ Store concept sounds. I'm off that now.

**Danny:** I didn't think you were serious anyway.

**Rex:** I was. It's built on a solid concept. It may be a lot to bring it to fruition, though. Not only are you going to have to deal with the technical issues of developing the software to support the idea, you also have to reeducate consumers. When they see a $40.00 hat marked 1,000, they need to realize that's 1,000 four cent charges, not $1,000. The sticker shock situation is the only real hurdle. I'm sure legally it's solid. The IT could be developed.

Consumer are fickle. Do they really want to re-learn everything they have ever known about retail pricing? That, my friend, I don't know. Nor does anyone else. I've come up with a groundbreaking approach to retail. I am sure it will happen one day, I'm just not sure consumers are ready for it now. With that in mind, I have a completely different idea, and it involves you.

**Danny:** Oh no. Did you steal my Cartoos idea and now you want to hire me to do all of the work?

**Rex:** No. I have already told you I'm not stealing that idea. This is better than that. Way better. One word: movie.

**Danny:** Like *Jurassic Park*?

**Rex:** Well, like *Jurassic Park* in that *Jurassic Park* was a movie. I mean you are talking a big budget Hollywood movie created in the Hollywood machine, directed by a Hollywood legend in Steven Spielberg. I'm talking a little more low-key. More along the lines of an independent breakout.

**Danny:** So you are going to write it, and how would this involve me?

**Rex:** No man. I wrote it. I actually stayed up all night last night. I was so fired up after our talk. I wrote a script. It just flowed, and it is unbelievable. We have to get it made. I can't do it alone, though. I need you, buddy!

**Danny:** You wrote a story?

**Rex:** No, I wrote a script. A movie script to be exact. I found how to format it on the internet. It's written. I've reread it several times. This is ready to be made.

**Danny:** What's the concept?

**Rex:** It's a superhero movie.

**Danny:** An independent superhero movie? That wouldn't work. These things are grandiose! The biggest of the blockbusters. I don't think we need another superhero movie, by the way.

**Rex:** This is different.

**Danny:** How so?

**Rex:** Number one, the superhero is a woman. Yes, there have been a few women superheroes, but I think you would agree females are grossly underrepresented in the genre.

**Danny:** Okay, I will make that concession. Not enough females.

**Rex:** Secondly, my superhero doesn't embrace her super powers like they do in all of the movies I have seen. Realizing the use of super powers means you give up a normal life and become some sort of crime fighting person in the public domain, she shuns it. Ultimately, she works a normal job and uses her super powers of 100 times the strength and speed of a normal woman to do random acts of kindness.

**Danny:** Random acts of kindness?

**Rex:** She makes the world a better place not putting crazy villains in funny costumes in jail, she puts her unique abilities to help society. Like in this one scene, she's got this single mother in her neighborhood who's really struggling with balancing home, family and maintaining a house. There are literally jobs like mowing the grass and landscaping she had never done. One day she comes home and Kendall Beckinsail has mowed the lawn, fixed the timber wall and roofed the house.

**Danny:** Whoa, whoa, whoa. She's not like Wonder Woman or something. She's Kendall Beckinsail?

**Rex:** Yes. Remember, she shuns the superhero lifestyle. She's just a normal woman.

**Danny:** So her superhero strength is she's good with lawn care?

**Rex:** That's just an example of someone with these strangely unique abilities to help others. I mean she does some cool stuff, too. She helps a baby out of a burning car after a car accident. She's just not going to become this person who gives up their whole life to be at the whims of some city who can't seem to have any control over criminals wearing costumes 24/7.

**Danny:** What's her costume look like?

**Rex:** Like yoga pants and a Grateful Dead t-shirt?

**Danny:** She likes the Grateful Dead?

**Rex:** Well… I can't say I went into the description of her outfits in the script, but in my mind she just wears normal clothes.

**Danny:** How did she acquire her super powers?

**Rex:** Actually, she goes on a vacation to Hawai'i where she set out to not do any touristy-type of traveling but instead embracing the history of the Hawaiian people by visiting only the spiritual places from Native Hawaiian culture. When she returns home, she notices this unusual new strength. She hadn't noticed it in Hawai'i since her powers are only active when she isn't on a Hawaiian Island. There is no need for these super powers there since the aumakua take care of you while you are in the motherland of Hawai'i. The story ends with her finding this out and choosing a normal life over that of a superhero by moving to Hawai'i.

**Danny:** Aumakua?

**Rex:** Gods.

**Danny:** So what's the name of this superhero movie?

**Rex:** *Kapu Powers*.

**Danny:** What does that mean?

**Rex:** Kapu is the Hawaiian word for forbidden. The powers are forbidden since she doesn't use them… at least not out in public.

**Danny:** I mean I guess this sounds like an interesting premise?

**Rex:** So you're in with me?

**Danny:** What does that mean? I'm making a movie with you?

**Rex:** Yeah, we take some time off of work and go pitch the movie to a few studios?

The guys grab their lunches and continue talking.

**Danny:** I'm not taking time off of work for this. I mean how do you think you are going to get in to see the heads of studios to get your project green-lighted? Or is it green-lit?

**Rex:** I'm not sure. I think both work. Anyway, I thought it could be something we could both work on together. I told you if I had an extra million I would give it to you. Here's an extra million. This has the potential to be huge. What do you have to lose?

**Danny:** My job! Plus, I just started over with my life when I moved down here, now I'm chasing a movie dream?

**Rex:** We'll do this, and we'll keep our jobs. This will be a side thing, until we hit it big. Then we don't need to worry about pronouncing Koki'o Ke'okeo.

**Danny:** All right. I guess you need to let me see the script. If it sounds good, I'll give this a try.

Not skipping a beat, Danny and Rex finish their lunch and then get back on planting the mound of plants Sam Māhoe has left for them. Of course, in the world of Danny Bandera and Rex Palakiko more working equals more talking.

**Danny:** Have you thought about your female lead? The role of Kendall Beckinsail probably makes or breaks this movie. Also, is there a male lead in your story?

**Rex:** Yes, there is a male lead. I will be playing him.

**Danny:** You can't act.

**Rex:** Sure I can. I'm a natural. Plus, I wrote this character, no one could bring the passion I bring to the Captain Donovan.

**Danny:** So you're a superhero, too?

**Rex:** No, Captain Donovan is just a normal guy.

**Danny:** So is he a boat captain, pilot, member of the military?

**Rex:** No, he's just a guy who happens to have the first name Captain, and, he's dating someone who happens to be a superhero. He knows about Kendall Beckinsail's unique powers but he's on the down low about them, too, since he doesn't want to lose her to the fame a superhero receives. I mean Kendall Beckinsail is a catch. She's charming, funny, a purveyor of good deeds and she's smoking hot.

**Danny:** Hold on, I'm now just realizing I'm risking my job by trying to help a guy who writes a movie where some guy is named Captain. What have I done with my life? Anyway, okay, who do you see playing Kendall Beckinsail… the girlfriend of Captain Donovan, and, in-turn, the de-facto girlfriend of Rex Palakiko.

**Rex:** See, when you say it like that, you make it seem weird. I don't want to get into it now.

**Danny:** No way. I'm a major contributor of this project I need to know.

**Rex:** Okay, okay. It's going to beeeeeeeeee....

**Danny:** Come on man. Out with it.

**Rex:** Kendall Beckinsail is going to be played by Jennifer Lawrence.

**Danny (laughing hysterically):** Okay, I'm done. You and I had a good run in the movie business but it's officially over now.

**Rex:** You don't like Jennifer Lawrence?

**Danny:** Are you kidding me? Jennifer Lawrence is it. There is no one hotter in terms of career, nor is there anyone hotter in terms of looks. She is the currency of Hollywood. Plus, despite all of the success, the big films, the awards and the non-stop scrutiny, she seems oddly normal. I mean you could go on a date with Gwyneth Paltrow, and it seems like for dinner she would order a bowl of raw unprocessed whole grain and milk from a single sourced cow who only listens to music from the baroque period and then wonder why the restaurant doesn't have it. In the meantime, I'm sitting next to her thinking I don't even know what the baroque era is. Jennifer Lawrence, on the other hand, would order a bowl of macaroni and cheese. Now that, my friend, is hot.

**Rex:** So you just made all of my points for me. I like when you disagree with me and then support my side of the argument.

**Danny:** I'm against your lame attempt to cast her because Jennifer Lawrence is exactly that way which makes your project an impossibility. She has an unlimited supply of opportunities. She might be interested in working small and independent occasionally, but you are too small and too independent. You've never made a movie. You'd never get the chance to get close enough to her to have her read it. Plus, even if you did, she's not going to work with some unknown guy.

**Rex:** You said she's oddly normal. Maybe we could bump into her at a diner. Maybe she just likes me for who I am. Look at this face. I've got an honest face. Hey, once we're acting together as boyfriend and girlfriend, who knows where it goes from there. Maybe I'm buying her macaroni and cheese.

**Danny:** No way, man. You need to go a little further down the food chain.

**Rex:** Kate Upton?

**Danny:** Are you kidding me? Have you not heard a word I have said?

**Rex:** She's single, too.

**Danny:** This has nothing to do with marital status. If they have opportunities readily available to them, they aren't going to go with an unknown. You, my friend, are unknown. At least in the world of Hollywood. Yes, in the world of Koki'o Ke'okeo you are legend, but Hollywood not so much.

**Rex:** Hey, Koki'o Ke'okeo, much better. So who do you suggest for my female lead?

**Danny:** If you are going to get a celebrity, someone who is known, you are going to have to look in the background. Someone who is on a TV show, or in the movies, who hasn't had a breakout role. There are good actresses out there like that who may like the idea of being a lead in small film, but you will need to do your homework.

**Rex:** Hey, I am committed to this. I think I will get one shot at making a movie so I want it to be the best effort possible.

**Danny:** You know, there are a few people who might be able to help us.

**Rex:** Who?

**Danny:** The first one is Cas Schwabe, a business owner I met at the Hanalei Farmers Market. She owns the Akamai Juice Company. She's had an unbelievable life. While in college she got the job as a stand-in for the main star on a movie, and she began working in films. Sometimes on camera, sometimes on the crew and other times in craft services.

**Rex:** Craft services?

**Danny:** Yes, she's a chef.

**Rex:** I hear they eat well on the sets of movies.

**Danny:** That's what Cas says. Basically, anything goes for the big stars. The great thing is Cas has maintained these friendships with these big time A-list Hollywood Stars.

**Rex:** Like who?

**Danny:** Matthew McConaughey, Woody Harrelson, Anthony Kiedis of the Red Hot Chili Peppers. All kinds of people. She cooks for many of them when they come to Kaua'i.

**Rex:** Whoa. This is all we need. We could get Matthew McConaughey to play my best friend. I mean there's not a part in the script right now, but I could work something in for Matthew!

**Danny:** Well, don't go reworking your script just yet. We'll need to talk with Cas and find out what she thinks about this. The good news is we start at Ha'ena State Park tomorrow. She's in Kilauea so she's pretty close. We could go see her at lunch.

**Rex:** Yeah, this sounds promising. Even if she can't land McConaughey for us she may have some ideas to help out. Maybe she happens to know Jennifer Lawrence.

**Danny:** Yeah, I'm sure. The other person you need to talk to is Kiki Davis.

**Rex:** Who's that?

**Danny:** Kiki Davis works for the State of Hawai'i, too. She works in the General Administration office. She's at the Punchbowl office in Honolulu. She handles all of the contracts and permits for companies filming in Hawai'i.

**Rex:** Do you know her?

**Danny:** No.

**Rex:** How do you know she does this?

**Danny:** I heard a couple of the guys talking about her at one of our First Thursday meetings. She's a big deal, too. Hawai'i has a pretty solid amount of TV and movie work. Not a single frame is shot without Kiki signing off on it. I'll bet she knows the right people to talk to.

**Rex:** Wow, you are adding something to this project. See, I'm glad I brought you in!

**Danny:** The great news is our timing is perfect. We are going to Honolulu to meet with the Park's team there about their park clean-up efforts. We can drive over to the Punchbowl office and meet Kiki on Monday afternoon.

Rex: That is perfect. I am feeling really good about our ability to make this movie happen. ***Kapu Powers*** all the way!

As they look around they see a courthouse ensconced in beautiful flowers and foliage. Everything has been planted, and the boys are ready to head home. As they pack up everything back onto the trailer, the inevitable question comes from Danny, "Pa'u hana pupus beer?" Rex surprised Danny with a response of, "Not tonight. My mind is racing. I've got work to do! By the way, you should get some aloe. You are sunburnt!"

At 6:07 a.m. the next morning, Danny's phone rang. He looked at his phone and Rex's picture was on his screen along with his number. He picked it up and greeted his friend and co-worker inquisitively.

**Danny:** Rex, what's up?

**Rex:** Hey man, you have to come by my place. Right now. Before work.

**Danny:** You sound a little frazzled. What's going on?

**Rex:** I'm just supercharged on Kona. I've been up most of the night working on something for the movie. I have to show it to you, though.

**Danny:** All right. I'll be by.

Approximately ten minutes later there was a knock at Rex's door. Rex yelled, "Come on in," and Danny opened up the door. He was surprised to see Rex had rearranged his entire studio apartment. Everything was shifted to one side of the room to free up access to a wall which ran the entire length of his place. On this wall, everything had been removed and now was replaced by pictures from the internet of female celebrities Rex had apparently printed. There was some sort of organization to the layout, but Danny wasn't sure of exactly what he was looking at.

**Danny:** Whoa, what is this? The new K-Tel At-Home Stalker Kit?

**Rex:** What do you mean? You are really sunburnt by the way. Lobster-like. It got way more intense after you left the courthouse job yesterday.

**Danny:** Hey, my neck appreciated the break. The hat's going back on, though. Anyway, this room you have set up is more than a little creepy, my friend. This is the sort of thing the FBI typically finds in someone's house who also happens to have a dungeon and a cemetery in their backyard or under their porch.

**Rex:** It's not like that at all. I took your advice.

**Danny:** My advice?

**Rex:** Yes, absolutely. I have taken a tactical approach to establishing who the female lead will be in our *Kapu Powers*.

**Danny:** Printed photos on your wall is a "tactical approach?" There are easily more than 100 pictures here.

**Rex:** Hey, I am thorough. What I have done is taken a realistic look at female celebrities and scored them on several parameters. These include acting ability, age, career success, where they are currently at in their career in terms of being at the high, mid or low point, physical fitness since they will be playing a superhero and, finally, ability to star in a comedic role. Even though this isn't a comedy, our starlet will have to deliver some snarky lines. Oh yeah, I did include natural beauty and gave bonus points for being single.

**Danny:** So, if they are really busy, with a great career, that's a low score?

**Rex:** Well, that's one parameter. It's weighted pretty heavy, for sure, but there are all of those other parameters which factor in, as well.

**Danny:** So Kathy Bates makes your list?

**Rex:** Well she does… kind of. She's the low end benchmark. Any time you are doing any type of scoring where there is a winner, there also must be the flipside of it. Unfortunately for Ms. Bates, she's the low end.

**Danny:** She's had a pretty good career. I'd say there is still demand for her out there in the right role.

**Rex:** Yes, but not this one. She scored decent, as you mentioned, in career-related factors, but age, physical fitness and a few other elements were simply too much for her to overcome.

**Danny:** So as you move to the right from Kathy Bates, you are going up your scale.

**Rex:** Correct.

**Danny:** So why is Uma so low?

**Rex:** You are forgetting everything you taught me. She isn't doing this project. I mean I love Uma. She may very well sit near the top of woman I would want to date, I know she's not starring in *Kapu Powers*.

**Danny:** Okay, moving forward. Bar Refaeli?

**Rex:** Can't act.

**Danny:** Lindsay Lohan?

**Rex:** Too much of a handful on the set.

**Danny:** Who's Abbie Cornish?

**Rex:** Yeah, that's the point. She's hot but not so much so to pull her up beyond where she sits based on all of the other parameters.

**Danny:** Halle Berry and Gwyneth Paltrow are apparently tied?

**Rex:** That's correct. Halle has already done the superhero thing, and Gwyneth, well, I had a special penalty applied to her for simply being annoying.

**Danny:** Okay, here's a mistake.

**Rex:** What do you mean?

**Danny:** Look how low Hayden Panettiere scored.

**Rex:** Well, I figured I don't know how to pronounce her last name, there is no way I can have her in the movie.

**Danny:** There is no provision for last name pronunciations in your system.

**Rex:** These measurements aren't set in granite. As a judge you have to have flexibility to factor in items which may negatively impact the success of the movie. Having me mispronouncing her name on the set is a problem. Therefore, I was proactive and fixed it before it happened.

**Danny:** How about just calling her by her character's name.

**Rex:** She's not Daniel Day-Lewis, walking around on set not breaking character. You shouldn't question this stuff you should just be pleased I'm taking this seriously.

**Danny:** Let's see some of your others... just running through the highlights now: Emma Stone, Rihanna, Taylor Schilling, Kate Upton, Jennifer Lawrence...

**Rex:** See, you probably thought I would have Kate or Jennifer at number one. I've embraced the Danny Bandera approach.

**Danny:** What's your issue with Scarlett Johansson?

**Rex:** The headlines of ScarJo and RexMo seemed too annoying.

**Danny (shaking his head at ScarJo/RexMo):** Diane Guerro?

**Rex:** Close, but a little too short.

**Danny:** Blake Lively?

**Rex:** The marriage to Ryan Reynolds bit her.

**Danny:** Sitting at number two, Jackie Cruz?

**Rex:** Yes, almost perfect. She's single, beautiful, talented, but despite all of this, she was just nosed out by number one.

**Danny:** Gina Dash? I thought she was a singer?

**Rex:** She is. What put her over the hump was she was born in Hawai'i. Her dad was in the military and she lived in O'ahu until she was three. She can act, too, though. I've seen her in two movies playing small roles. She was the sister of Reese Witherspoon, who scored low based on her "cuteness" in my rankings by the way, in the movie *The Empire State*. She was also a heroin junkie in *Nature's Depravity*, an independent movie where she had a bigger role. Didn't do much at the box office, but I'm telling you she was good. She seems to be the perfect person to take on a starring role in our independent film. Plus, her Wikipedia page says she's single.

**Danny:** Again, why does that matter? Seriously!

**Rex:** Hey, we are playing boyfriend and girlfriend on screen. I need for this to be real life. I need to want this woman. So much so, it's probably going to carry over into our personal lives. What can we do?

**Danny:** Well, as odd and somewhat scary as I think this is, I believe you have put in some due diligence here. I don't think just vetting out and hanging a photo on a wall lands you Gina Dash for the movie, but at least you are thinking. I'm going to take off and grab a coffee. I will meet you at Ha'ena State Park. Don't forget we're going to see Cas Schwabe at lunch. I called her last night and said we would like to talk to her about the movie business. She said we could come by at lunch.

**Rex:** Sounds good. I hope Cas can help us out. See you there!

At 7:58 a.m. Rex pulled into Ha'ena State Park, and he could already see Danny Bandera's Elantra on the parking lot. He parked next to Danny's car and exited his Jeep to find Danny nearby surveying the area.

**Danny:** I think this is pretty simple. We are going to want to start our clean up over there at the edge of the beach and work our way across and back, piling up all trash right in front of this parking lot. It's an open area not really used so it makes the project pretty unobtrusive for visitors since we're keeping this place open during clean up and construction.

**Rex:** Sounds good. They already have a barrier in the water so we don't need to worry about that. Are we refreshing the sand here? It looks like there is some erosion needing to be dealt with.

**Danny:** Yes, that's part of the project. There will be some new sand brought in. We'll need to replace the entrance sign and get this parking lot restriped as well. We'll remove all of the weeds and get some new plants in here. This place will look like new when we are done.

**Rex:** All right, let's get started on some trash duty. I've got the bags and rakes for us in my Jeep.

As they get started, Rex gets the casual conversation going by inquiring what Danny did last night while he was holed up in his apartment, working on his female costar scoring system.

**Rex:** So Danny, since we didn't pa'u hana last night, what did you end up doing?

**Danny:** Well, I called this girl I met at the Hanalei Farmers Market.

**Rex:** Another woman met at the Farmers Market?

**Danny:** Yes, there is more than just fresh produce at the Farmers Market. Now you know why I'm really going there every weekend.

**Rex:** So you called this woman…

**Danny:** Yes. Danielle Keawe. I mean it was Saturday night, my buddy abandoned me for pa'u hana fun, so I just figured I'd call and talk to her. I call her and she answers. I figured we're off to a good start. We get to talking, and she says she's hungry. I'm thinking that's a decent hint she wants to go to dinner so I ask her out.

**Rex:** What did she say?

**Danny:** The good news was she said 'yes.'

**Rex:** Is there bad news?

**Danny:** She suggested Wrangler's Steakhouse.

**Rex:** What's wrong with Wrangler's Steakhouse? I like that place!

**Danny:** I mean it's right by her house. I'm thinking that's a bad sign. It's really convenient for her, but I'm in Līhue, like 45 minutes away. If she was interested, would she want to go to a place that was easy for both of us? Of course, I act like it's just right around the corner and accept her invitation.

**Rex:** So this chick is hot.

**Danny:** Of course. I'm not driving from Līhue to Waimea for a toad. So I make an excuse about seeing a friend, and then I'll meet her at the restaurant at 6:30.

**Rex:** You didn't pick her up.

**Danny:** I figure that's my insurance policy. I don't want to get stuck with the bill if this isn't a real date.

I figure if I'm not picking her up it could either be a friend's dinner or a date dinner. I'll just grab the bill if it goes well and act like that was always the plan from the start. So I arrive and it starts out great. I mean she's looking incredible. I'm thinking this is now a date…

**Rex:** Now it's a date because she looks good?

**Danny:** Sure. She looked so good my mindset was I'm lucky she's talking to me. If I can make this a date, even if she didn't initially intend it to be, the better off I am. I maybe be able to parlay this into boyfriend status before she realizes she's way out of my league. Of course, now I'm trying to impress so I order the lobster tail with my steak.

**Rex:** Time out. How does this supposedly impress her?

**Danny:** I mean I don't know for sure. There's just some voice in my head saying if you order steak and lobster, it looks like you really have it together. It's like going on a job interview to a casual company in a suit. You're trying to dress up to get the job. I was trying to eat beyond my means to look like I could apply for the job of being Danielle's boyfriend.

**Rex:** Job? See, that comment alone makes me think your priorities are so messed up you don't have a chance here. Secondly, don't you get sick when you eat lobster?

**Danny:** Well, that's what I've found. You never know these things for sure. I mean what if I happened to get bad lobster each time I had ordered it in the past? Does that mean I should never enjoy something most people find incredibly enjoyable because I was unlucky enough to get some bad lobster? What if they didn't cook it right? What if I happened to be sick already when I was eating it and the symptoms didn't manifest until after I ate the lobster?

**Rex:** There can be cases when there is too much of the benefit of a doubt. This might be one. I would say if you get sick every time you eat lobster, quit eating lobster!

**Danny:** It might not even be the lobster. Maybe it's the drawn butter?

**Rex:** Drawn butter?

**Danny:** The stuff they serve with lobster. They call it drawn butter. I don't actually even know what it is.

**Rex:** It's butter.

**Danny:** No it's not. It's some sort of butter-like liquid they only serve with lobster.

**Rex:** Yes, it's melted butter.

**Danny:** Then they would call it melted butter. They call it drawn butter. I don't care if you order lobster in Hawai'i, St. Louis, or Maine, they serve it with drawn butter.

**Rex:** Yes, melted butter goes good with lobster.

**Danny:** Then why don't they say corn on the cob and drawn butter? They always say melted butter with corn on the cob. I'm telling you it's different.

**Rex:** It is not.

**Danny:** I've tasted plenty of drawn butter. Oddly, it always tastes the same. Melted butter, on the other hand seems to vary greatly by the brand.

**Rex:** So, did you eat your lobster tail with melted butter?

**Danny:** No. I did get a mini ear of corn on the cob and enjoyed that with melted butter which tasted entirely different from the drawn butter I was dunking my lobster tail into.

**Rex:** So you're eating butter in several forms, living the high life by eating lobster with an admittedly smoking hot woman. How could this possibly have gone wrong?

**Danny:** Well, I would say there never is a great time to start talking about your cats, but if I could do the female population a great service, I would suggest never bringing it up on the first date.

**Rex:** So, crazy cat lady-ish?

**Danny:** Absolutely. Plus, she had this strong opinions how her kids were going to be raised.

**Rex:** First date… kids?

**Danny:** Oh yeah. Just insane stuff, too. They are only wearing plain white outfits so advertisers do not get to them too young. No TV. Minimal carbs. No sweets. I'll be honest, I tuned her out halfway through dinner. Just trying to power through the conversation and my steak and lobster.

**Rex:** And drawn butter.

**Danny:** Yes, my drawn butter, as well.

**Rex:** So how does all of this end?

**Danny:** Well, the waiter comes by and sets the bill down. She was closest to him so he happened to place it near Danielle. She tells me to look at this couple making out behind us, so, as I turn, I see her gently pushing the bill towards me. That was it. The final straw. I think I could have gotten through the rest since she was so stunning, but this move was just too much.

**Rex:** Did you pay?

**Danny:** Of course. At this point it's almost like a divorce, and I just want out, so I strategize the best way to do it cleanly is to pay this bill. If she ever calls me again, I don't owe her a thing. I went to dinner with her, I bought. I don't want to see her anymore. This is the end of the story. The wild thing was I came to dinner with $163.00 in my pocket. The bill as $131.26. I was terrified I wouldn't have enough as I looked down at the bill.

**Rex:** You didn't have a credit card? Plus, $131.26 sounds a little steep for the two of you. Was that total correct?

**Danny:** Between my steak and lobster and these expensive drinks she kept ordering, it added up pretty quickly. I have a credit card, but I don't usually carry it. It's too easy to spend when you've got the easy access to money through one of those cards. Luckily, I had enough cash and I gave the waiter $160.00, said goodbye to Danielle and then I left.

**Rex:** No kiss?

**Danny:** Absolutely not. I mean that wasn't even on the table. It was a polite goodbye. I didn't set any expectation of a phone call or future date. I simply told her I would see her at Hanalei Farmers Market sometime.

**Rex:** Wow, $160 is a pretty steep "leave me alone" buyout when you consider this was a one date relationship.

**Danny:** You're telling me.

**Rex:** So, it was a pretty bad night.

**Danny:** Well, it gets worse.

**Rex:** How so? Did she call you?

**Danny:** No, I haven't heard from her. Like 5 minutes out of Waimea, I get this twinge in my bowels. That lobster… or that drawn butter… whatever it is was getting me again.

**Rex:** So what did you do?

**Danny:** Well, I thought I would press on. Just power my way through the pain and get home. About five more minutes in I knew nature wasn't going to wait. There isn't a lot between Waimea and Līhue, so when I got to Kalāheo, I knew I had to stop. It was like 9:00, though. Almost everything was shut down. Stores, restaurants, even some bars I saw… all closed for the night. I see this one restaurant that looked open. I had never heard of it before. Some Thai restaurant. I pull in, car askew in my haste and just tear in there. The whole time I'm just praying as I walk in that there is a bathroom. If there is, I'll make a bee line for it and then deal with the consequences when I leave. I'll just tell the manager or owner I'm not interested in eating there and leave. There won't be much they can do to me… as long as I get the chance to burn a mule in there I'm fine.

**Rex:** Burn a mule?

**Danny:** You know, chopping butt wood, building a log cabin, colon bowlin'!

**Rex (laughing):** This was serious.

**Danny:** So, I open the door, I'm crestfallen. There is a guy waiting for me. He's got a menu in his hand and is asking me if it is just one dining tonight. I said, 'table for two I'm waiting for someone. I need to use the bathroom, though, while I wait.' The guy pointed me towards the restroom but I had already spotted it and was heading that way.

**Rex (laughing harder):** Wait, wait. Why did you say table for two?

**Danny:** Well, I just had eaten. I doubt he was going to let me just use the bathroom without dining. There was no way I was staying for another dinner so a table for two was my way out. When my "friend" didn't show up, I could bail.

**Rex:** Not bad.

**Danny:** I know, right? So the problem here was the fact there were only two people in this tiny restaurant. There is just a single bathroom for men and women, and it's a door in the dining room. The one couple in there is at a table right outside of the door. As I open the door, I realize they are like 7 feet from where I will be sitting on the throne and the door is pretty thin. Like a builder grade closet door. Normally, I would be embarrassed by the potential of them hearing, and worse smelling what is about to happen, but, I'm at the point of no return here. I didn't care at that moment. Not one bit.

I go into the bathroom. As I'm unbuttoning my shorts I can hear the couple outside of the door talking. They are debating what they are getting for dinner. The woman wants the man to get a certain thing so she can share it…(stops talking).

**Rex:** What? Why did you stop?

**Danny:** Because that's the last thing I heard before I unleashed the kraken. The closest experience I can relate this to was when I was a kid and we went to a civil war battle reenactment. I can still remember not only the sound of the cannon battles but the feeling. The ground seemed to reverberate, shaking your body with each cannon fire. This was like that. I mean I destroyed that bathroom. Just unleashing round after round of thunder boomers (Note: Rex is laughing to the point of tears). The echo of those gastric expulsions blasting in that porcelain chamber was something to behold. It was a sensory experience of sights, sounds, smells and feelings. I finished up, washed my hands and took my seat wondering what that couple was now saying with me being out of the bathroom.

**Rex (tears streaming down his cheeks):** Oh my. So many questions. Why are you sitting down? You already ate. You had your way out. That fake story of the person you were waiting for.

**Danny:** Well, I couldn't just leave. I had to act like I was waiting for someone, so I sat down and ordered a soda. Then I remembered I only had $3 on me. I quickly checked the menu and a soda cost $2.99. I'm checking my phone a lot so it looks like I'm watching the time or looking for text messages. In reality I'm trying to remember if I have any change in the car to cover the tax and tip for this soda.

**Rex:** So how does this end?

**Danny:** After about ten minutes I walked up and told the owner it looked like my friend wasn't showing up and I needed to square up with him for the soda. He was like just forget it, so I headed out and went home.

**Rex:** So did you learn anything?

**Danny:** Oh, I'm off the lobster. No more experimenting or thinking it's something else. No lobster for me… ever!

**Rex:** Hey, it's lunch time. Let's stop where we are at and go see Cas.

**Danny:** Sounds good.

Like most, Cas Schwabe's career path was established in college, it's just she took a little more unconventional road to get there than most. While attending college in Virginia, the miniseries ***A Woman Named Jackie*** was filming nearby. Cas went to the set and inquired about work and ended up securing the position as Roma Downey's assistant (the lead actress in the movie). During the filming Cas not only gained experience working in movie production, she also made some invaluable connections.

Her contacts led to several more jobs in the entertainment industry including some on-screen work. The best connections she made, though, were with the caterers on the sets of these projects. Her family had owned a restaurant, so she had always been around the food industry growing up. The complexity of working craft services on a movie set appealed to her. Early on she noted the chefs for the caterers in movie productions have to be equally adept at making high end cuisine for the unique demands of the big stars as they are at running a chow line for the rest of the cast, crew and press on the set.

Cas enjoyed the pressure of creating specialty crafted meals for the A-listers as much as she did creating a flavorful buffet for the masses. Her cooking was so good, it became a coveted acting gig to be on the set of a Cas Schwabe catered set.

Her standout work as a chef led to friendships with some high powered individuals and some of the most well-known celebrities in business. All of this came at a price, though. The long hours, unreliable staff and sporadic nature of the movie industry took a toll on Cas' health and mental well-being.

She decided to walk away from the movie business and start over in Kaua'i. Compared to the grind of Hollywood, living in the tropical paradise of Hawai'i seemed like a dream.

Initially, Cas pursued a different passion in Kaua'i. She decided to become a helicopter pilot. Since the economy was struggling the cost of getting lessons was a stretch at $250 an hour, but still in the reach of someone totally committed to the craft.

Cas jumped in with the enthusiasm she had taken to everything in her life and became certified to fly helicopters. In doing so, she became the first female helicopter pilot on Kaua'i. As the economy picked up, the demand for pilots increased which may seem good, but for Cas it actually negatively impacted her ability to make a living. She would need ongoing training to continue to maintain her license and learn to operate other machines. With the demand for pilots so strong, the cost for training jumped to $750 an hour.

Cas realized she couldn't afford to keep flying so she began to look for yet another career path. Her search led her back to a twist on what she knew best: cooking. One of her specialties as a caterer to the stars had been unique smoothie and juice concoctions. She began to sell her creations at the Hanalei Farmers Market, close to her home in Kilauea. The response was so strong from the very first weekend she set up a booth, she knew she was onto something.

She began to expand by offering in-home delivery to customers. She also supplemented her income further by selling to hotels and resorts looking to offer a flavor of Hawai'i at their breakfast tables with Cas' juices. As she expanded beyond the Farmers Market, she began selling under the brand name of the Akamai Juice Company.

The whole time Cas was working as a helicopter pilot, and starting her juice company, she stayed active as a caterer serving as a personal chef to her many celebrity friends who came to Kaua'i for a visit. When they would come for vacation, she would make easy-to-prepare meals they could simply "heat and eat."

Danny Bandera met Cas during his weekly Saturday visit to the Hanalei Farmers Market. Initially, he was drawn to her booth from the colorful Akamai Juice Company "trucker style" baseball hats she sold. These unique caps were hand-designed individually by Kaua'i artist Maxine Graham. The hats have an almost cult-like following with Cas' celebrities pals being spotted wearing them all over the world.

After initially talking with Cas about her hats and celebrity friends, he quickly became a fan of her juices and smoothies. To this day, his favorite remains her Cucumber Mint Slushy, which she makes right on site at her Hanalei Farmers Market booth.

When Rex came up with the idea of making a movie, Danny immediately began to think Cas might play some role in being able to help them out. The boys arrived at the production facility for her juice company. Cas and Danny hugged, and he introduced Rex to Cas. Expecting their visit, Cas surprised her guests with some fish tacos and juice for lunch. They sat down, and the conversation started.

**Cas:** Wow, Danny. Your face is really badly sunburned.

**Danny:** Yeah, I had an issue with the sun at one of our jobs. I'm on a pretty aggressive aloe therapeutic program now.

**Rex:** Cas, do you have any chili water for these tacos?

**Cas:** Of course I do. I make it myself.

**Rex (pouring a little on a spoon and sampling it):** Hey, not bad. I love this stuff. When I was growing up on Kaua'i, there wasn't a home on the island which didn't have their homemade version of chili water in their refrigerator. Same thing for restaurants. It was on every table. Now you struggle to find it. I've actually started carrying it with me into restaurants.

**Danny:** Cas, you have worked in craft services on the set of movies, right?

**Cas:** Absolutely.

**Danny:** What's the food like on the set of a movie?

**Cas:** Depending on the movie, it can be insane. Like a five star restaurant for hundreds of people. Everyone ate good on the set of any movie I was involved with, that's for sure.

**Rex:** I understand through your time in the movie business you have maintained a lot of connections even as you left the industry.

**Cas:** Well, I've either worked on or in dozens of movies. Mostly as a chef and caterer, but I have had several minor roles, as well. Over the course of my career, I made many long-lasting friendship and you are correct, many I still stay in touch with today.

**Rex:** I wrote a movie called *Kapu Powers*.

**Cas:** Forbidden powers, right?

**Rex:** Exactly. Do you know Gina Dash?

**Danny:** Rex. Easy. We'll get into that in a moment. Why don't you tell her about the project?

**Rex:** Okay. Well, it's a superhero movie with a female superhero.

**Cas:** I like that.

**Rex:** I know. Not enough strong female superheroes. So we've got an animals script I wrote. I want to get the movie made, but I don't want to simply sell the script. I want to be involved, and, in fact, I would like to star in it as the boyfriend opposite of our female lead. We could really use some help.

**Cas:** Okay. I do a little Taekwando, some yoga and while my abs aren't shredded, I mean I'm in pretty good shape.

**Danny:** Um, Rex?

**Rex:** What we really need is help getting a kind of well-known, yet not-too-well-known lead. That gets back to the question, do you know Gina Dash?

**Cas:** The singer? No, I've never met her. I am good friends with the guys in the Red Hot Chili Peppers. Anthony Kiedes wears my hats to almost every Lakers game he attends.

**Rex:** Cool. Can you ask him for Gina's number? I want to reach out to her about the lead part in *Kapu Powers*.

**Cas:** I can't do that.

**Rex:** Why not, he's probably got it.

**Cas:** He probably does, or, at a minimum, knows someone who could get it. I just can't ask him. The reason why I have so many celebrity friends is the fact I treat them like friends, not celebrities. People ask them for everything. Can I get tickets to this… can I get tickets to that… can I, can I, can I? It becomes too much for them, and they draw inwards to a small circle of friends. I'm in that sort of inner circle relationship with these people, and I don't want to break that trust.

**Rex:** What about Matthew McConaughey?

**Cas:** I am great friends with Matthew. I not only cook for him whenever he comes to Kaua'i, he brings me on the set of his movies to be his personal chef. Again, though, I can't break his trust by asking him for favors.

**Rex:** No, not a favor, we want to hire him. He could be my older brother in the movie.

**Cas:** He doesn't look much like you.

**Rex:** It's a blended family thing.

**Danny:** I didn't see any "blended family thing" in the script.

**Rex:** Danny, stifle it. Adults are talking business here.

**Cas:** I'm sorry. I just don't talk this sort of business with Matthew. We talk about the beach, my juices, really anything but Hollywood and the industry.

**Danny:** Cas, it's okay. We understand. We do. Right, Rex?

**Rex:** Yeah sure, I guess. If I had a friend, though, I would like them to tell me if they had an opportunity for me to work.

**Danny:** Rex, in all honesty we still don't know how much of an opportunity we have here. I mean we haven't made a movie before. The way I see it, Cas is looking out for a friend.

**Rex:** Okay, okay. Cas, it was great meeting you. Loved the fish tacos, the Akamai juice and the chili water. I'm even going to buy a hat. Give me that one over there with the octopus. How is the juice business, by the way?

**Cas:** Well, it could be better. I've got the good kind of problems to have. My business has grown so fast I've outgrown my facility here. I need to get a new place but that's almost a full-time job just finding something. Eventually I will get around to it. I guess when I can't stand to be crammed in here anymore. In the meantime, I just need to get by.

**Rex (trying on his Octopus/Akamai Juice Company hat):** Hey, check it out.

**Cas:** It looks great.

**Danny:** Yes it does. Now you are cool. I have nine of her hats. She even had Maxine Graham, the artist she uses, make me a Grateful Dead Akamai Juice Hat. A true one-of-a-kind! Thanks so much for your time Cas.

**Cas:** Thanks guys.

Despite the fact their meeting with Cas did not go well, Rex and Danny were still enthused about their meeting tomorrow with Kiki Davis. She certainly had the connections they needed to make a movie.

They finished off their work at Ha'ena State Park and went straight home since they had an early flight scheduled to Honolulu the next day.

The next morning, Danny and Rex flew to Honolulu to meet with members of the O'ahu Parks and Recreations Department. They learned about some of the initiatives and successes they have achieved in cleaning up their parks. The two teams shared some ideas, and everyone walked away feeling better prepared to do their job.

As soon as their meeting was over, they headed over to the General Administration Office on Punchbowl Street in Honolulu. They walked up to the front desk and asked for Kiki Davis.

**Clerk at the Front Desk:** Is she expecting you?

**Rex and Danny:** No.

**Clerk at the Front Desk:** What is this in regard to?

**Rex:** We work for the State of Hawai'i as well. We work over in Kaua'i.

**Clerk at the Front Desk:** Oh, okay. I will let her know you are here (looking at the sign-in sheet). Just have a seat, Danny and Rex; she will be right with you.

A few minutes later, Kiki Davis appeared in the lobby. She introduced herself to Danny and Rex. They told her they needed to discuss a movie project so she welcomed them into her office.

Her office looked like it should be on the Sunset Strip. There were photos everywhere of celebrities posing with Kiki on the sets of films and TV shows being shot in Hawai'i.

**Kiki:** So you guys have a project coming to Kaua'i you need to discuss?

**Danny:** Well not actually… um. Well, it's like…

**Rex:** Ms. Davis.

**Kiki:** Kiki.

**Rex:** Kiki, what my silver-tongued friend is trying to say this isn't about a project coming to Kaua'i. There may be some key scenes filmed here, but we have a movie script I wrote called *Kapu Powers*. It's a superhero story we need help getting a production company involved.

**Kiki:** It's good?

**Rex:** This is unlike anything you've ever seen. It is awesome.

**Kiki:** You know I grew up on Kaua'i. Did you know Walter Palakiko?

**Rex:** That was my grandfather!

**Kiki:** Are you kidding me? Walter used to be friends with my father. They worked together.

**Rex:** It's true, Walter was my grandfather, and my hero. He taught me everything about life, he made me focus on my career, and he taught me how to make the best chili water.

**Kiki:** Yes, I sure would like to have some of the chili water my mother used to make. It was the best. Anyway, any relative of Walter Palakiko is a friend of mine. I know a guy named Chip Van der Dorr. He has his own production company, and he works with all of the large studios for promotion and distribution. If he can't get your movie made nobody can. Let's call him right now.

**Danny:** This sounds awesome. Let's do it.

**Rex:** Yeah, like right now. I mean right, right now. Kiki, pick up the phone.

Kiki smiles and picks up the phone and dials Chip Van der Dorr from memory. Whomever answered the phone recognized Kiki's voice and put her right through to Chip.

**Chip:** Kiki, my sweetie. What can I do for you? I'm hoping you are calling me to say you have all of the sign-offs for my next project?

**Kiki:** Not quite yet. It takes a while for these things. You know that, Chip.

**Chip:** I know, I know, Kiki. So what do I owe this wonderful call for, then?

**Kiki:** I have two guys in my office right now. Old friends from Kaua'i. They have a movie they've written and want to get made. I sure would appreciate if you could sit down and talk with them about it.

**Chip:** Kiki, I can't commit to making a movie sight unseen. You know how it works.

**Kiki:** I do know, Chip. I'm just asking you to see what they have and sit with them. These are young guys who haven't made a movie before. Even if this project isn't right for you, I'm guessing you could give them some really great advice about the movie business.

**Chip:** Sure thing Kiki. The only issues is I leave Wednesday to Vancouver for a movie shoot. I'm out six weeks. Can they meet with me tomorrow?

**Kiki (pushing the phone aside):** Chip wants to know if you could be in Los Angeles tomorrow for a meeting. He's going to be out of town starting Wednesday.

**Rex:** Tuesday is our day off. We can fly in and fly out and still be back to Kaua'i for work on Wednesday.

**Danny:** We can?

**Rex:** Absolutely. Tell Chip to book it.

**Kiki:** They are in. Rex and Danny, Chip wants to know if 10:00 a.m. tomorrow sounds okay?

**Rex:** Book it.

**Kiki:** Okay, Chip, put down Rex Palakiko and Danny Bandera down for 10:00 a.m. to discuss their movie *Kapu Powers*.

**Chip:** What does that mean?

**Kiki:** Forbidden powers. They will tell you all about it. Okay, Chip, take care.

**Chip:** Bye, honey. By the way, call me as soon as…

Kiki hangs up.

**Kiki:** I've got one favor to ask you guys now.

**Danny:** Sure. What do you need?

**Kiki:** If you end up shooting in Los Angeles, can my daughter Stella (pointing to a photo on the wall of an attractive young woman posing with Steven Spielberg on the set of the most recent Jurassic Park movie) come on the set? She is a senior film student at UCLA. Any experience she can get helps.

**Rex:** Sure thing. So she wants to get into the movie business?

**Kiki:** Yes, she grew up around it with me doing this job for so many years. I always took her on the sets. The funny thing was she always gravitated more towards the directors than the actors. She wants to be a filmmaker.

**Danny:** What a great school to learn about the industry. That's the Harvard of film schools.

**Kiki:** It is. It also seems to cost as much as Harvard. My husband and I have tried to pay everything as we went, but still, we are in $35,000 of debt. My husband works for the Health Department here. It's tough making it on a State salaries. We only have one child, though, so I guess we are trying to do it right.

**Rex:** It sounds like you are. If we should end up making this is Los Angles, we will be sure to give you a call to get in touch with Stella.

**Kiki:** Sounds good. Just give me a buzz if you need to reach her or anything else.

**Rex:** Kiki, one last thing (opening his briefcase). You will really appreciate this since you are from Kaua'i. It's two bottles of Līhue Barbecue's secret sauce. They don't sell it in stores.

**Kiki:** Like we used to say back when I was hanging out with friends in Kaua'i, 'roger that, brah!' Līhue Barbecue is the best. There is nothing like it on O'ahu. This is great. You didn't have to do that. I mean I really appreciate it, but you didn't need to bring a gift.

**Rex:** Come on, you know better. I'm not coming here asking for a favor without bringing a gift. It's like if you invite me to a cookout. I'm not coming with some chips and soda. I'm bringing pounds of poki. You have to not only bring a gift, but go the extra step to have some meaning.

**Kiki:** Well, I have to tell you, this is fantastic. We will be grilling tonight! Best of luck to both of you with your project.

The boys said goodbye to Kiki and headed out. There wasn't time to get home to Kaua'i so they picked up some clothes at the store and headed straight to the airport to catch an 8:30 p.m. flight. They were lucky to get the flights to work out perfectly, allowing them to make their meeting with Chip Van der Dorr and get back to Kaua'i in time to get to work on Wednesday.

They were both confident their journey of getting into the movie business was about to begin.

Rex and Danny grabbed some sleep on the plane since it would be the only rest they would get today. Between the long flight and the time change, and getting dressed at the airport, they were hitting the road in Los Angeles at 6:30 in the morning. They decided to stop at KJ's Diner near the airport to get some breakfast and discuss their strategy. After ordering their meal they got down to business.

**Danny:** Rex, this is our moment, but are we even ready for this? What's our approach here?

**Rex:** I have three copies of the script. One for me, one for you and one for Chip. We'll run through it with him. I know he's going to love it. Then it's just a matter of negotiating our deals. I'm hoping we can get this whole thing wrapped up today.

**Danny:** Okay. It sounds like you have this under control. I'll let you take the lead and chime in when you need me.

**Rex:** Hey, look over there in the corner. Sitting by herself, under the sunglasses and hat. That's Jennifer Lawrence, isn't it?

**Danny:** No way. I do think it's her. Look at what she's eating… it's just like what I said.

**Rex:** You said she would be eating macaroni and cheese. She's eating chicken and waffles.

**Danny:** It's breakfast you idiot. Chicken and waffles is the macaroni and cheese of breakfast.

**Rex:** How is this possible? It's 6:52 in the morning in a diner and Jennifer Lawrence is by herself. I've got the chicken skin, man.

**Danny:** Chicken skin?

**Rex:** Goosebumps. This is fate. We are destined to make this movie. Take that Gina Dash, we are getting Jennifer Lawrence to be in our movie.

**Danny:** Fate? She's eating breakfast.

**Rex:** On the same date, at the same time as we are preparing to pitch a movie we had her penciled in as the female lead. I mean how many restaurants are in L.A.? Tens of thousands? She is here right now. We are getting her in **Kapu Powers**. This was meant to be.

**Danny:** Okay. We both don't need to go rushing over there. She'll feel overwhelmed. It needs to just one. I will handle this.

**Rex:** Speaking to Jennifer Lawrence? You? No way. I've got this.

**Danny:** Absolutely not. I come across as more mature (pronounced "ma-tour" to emphasize his point).

**Rex:** Sure. An older creepy guy with a bunch of tattoos. Very calming.

**Danny:** Hey, you are handling the Van der Wazzer meeting or whatever that guy's name is. This one is mine. I'm a part of this movie, too. Plus, let's not forget you get a make out scene with her in the movie if she agrees to be in it. You will get plenty of interaction with her. This is my moment. This is my fate. I have chicken skin.

**Rex:** All right. By the way, those tattoos just look creepy with your chicken skin.

**Danny:** Thank you for noticing. Now, if you will excuse me, I need to go land an A-list celebrity for our movie.

Walking over to the table, Danny confirms without a doubt it really is Jennifer Lawrence. What a striking beauty. She's got the whole "hot chick" thing going on where she is trying to look hagged-out to ward off gawkers, yet, oddly, it makes her look that much more intriguing. This isn't "red carpet" Jennifer Lawrence, this is the Jennifer Lawrence who would be walking around Danny's apartment if they were dating. He started to get really nervous as he approached her table. Wanting to maintain her privacy, she never makes eye contact until he's standing right in front of her.

**Danny:** Ms. Lawrence, you don't know me but my name is…

**Jennifer Lawrence (interrupting):** Excuse me? I'm eating breakfast here.

**Danny:** I know, and I apologize. It's just that my associate and I (Rex waves with the enthusiasm of a child flagging down the ice cream truck), are a few hours from pitching our movie to a big muckety-muck in Hollywood.

**Jennifer Lawrence:** Muckety-muck?

**Danny:** Yeah, a big player here. We have a part for you…

**Jennifer Lawrence:** I don't want to hear it. Call my agent if you want to pitch a script.

**Danny:** But you're so normal. You are eating chicken and waffles. It's the macaroni and cheese of breakfast.

**Jennifer Lawrence:** Get out of here… NOW!

**Danny:** Let me get you a quick copy of the script. I am going to need it back for the meeting, though.

**Jennifer Lawrence:** If you don't leave, right now, I'm going to stand up and kick you right in the nuts.

**Danny:** Whoa, wait a minute. Can my associate film that? We're also working on a show called Nut Shots. You could appear in a celebrity edition segment.

With that, Jennifer Lawrence jumped up and drilled a size ten Jimmy Choo deep into Danny's hacky sack. He dropped to the floor like he'd been shot and thrashed around on the floor of KJ Diner trying to roll it off. Jennifer Lawrence marched right out the door, and Rex came racing over to check on his buddy.

**Rex:** Are you all right?

**Danny (gasping for breath):** Oh my god. Jennifer Lawrence touched my nuts! Sure, it wasn't exactly how I imagined it would be, but still, there was touching nonetheless. She's got perfect little toes. Even the baby toe had polish. You should have seen 'em.

**Rex:** So they only thing accomplished here was some nut touching? What was your agenda here? I'm guessing she's not in our movie.

**Danny:** I think she needs more time to think about it.

With that, the waitress came over with a check in her hand. "Hey, she didn't pay. I'm assuming you guys are picking up her meal?"

"Yes, I guess that is correct," replied Rex.

At 9:55 a.m., Rex and Danny strolled into Chip Van der Dorr's office. They checked-in at the front desk and took a seat in the waiting room. At 10:00, an assistant introduced herself and took them back to Chip's office. He was on the phone as they entered.

As he was finishing up his call, Danny and Rex made non-verbal rolling eye motions to one another as they noticed the coy and charming Chip they heard on the phone with Kiki wasn't the same attitude they were hearing right now. He was brash and direct. He hung up his phone and turned to Rex and Danny sitting in chairs on the other side of his desk.

**Chip:** Okay, what can I do for you clowns?

**Danny:** Clowns? I'm Danny Bandera and this is Rex Palakiko. We want to talk to you about…

**Chip:** I know, I know. You want to pitch a movie idea. That never happens to me. If I opened this door and said I'm listening to pitches, do you have any idea how long the line would be?

**Rex:** Long.

**Chip:** It would snake down to Tijuana where Border Patrol would cut it off for safety purposes.

**Rex:** I thought Kiki told you we have something pretty special here.

**Chip:** Kiki did talk to me. That's the only reason I'm talking to you. I've got a blockbuster shooting down in Hawai'i later this year. Without Kiki Davis, we're over before we get started. Hence my attentive and supportive meeting with you. So, Danny and Rex, you have my full attention for the next 30 minutes. Convince me you are the real deal and not a couple of donkeys who learned about how to write a script on the internet and thought they had the next Titanic on their hands.

**Rex:** We are going to surprise you here. Here's the script.

**Chip:** Okay.

**Rex:** Let's start on page one. *Kendall Beckinsail sits in her apartment pondering what she is doing with her life as she searches for vacation options for her and her boyfriend Captain Donovan. Her browser, detecting a vacation search in progress, has a pop-up ad for deals going to Hawai'i.*

**Chip:** Wait just a moment. Are you going sit there and read this entire script?

**Rex:** Yes. We're pitching you our movie.

**Chip:** (under his breath he emphatically says, "Kiki" and then shakes his head and begins speaking.) Listen, you guys are clueless how this works. You don't bring your script in and read it to someone who you are trying to get to invest in your vision. The script is a vehicle for the director to make the movie. You should be walking in with a treatment which is a synopsis of the story and then combine it with a passionate discussion as to why you want me to partner with you. Okay, forget the script. Tell me about your movie.

**Rex:** It's about a woman who goes to Hawai'i for vacation. She shuns the traditional touristy destinations on the islands and embraces the Native Hawaiian culture by visiting the sacred spots while her boyfriend sits on the beach. She ends up befriending a Native Hawaiian who appreciates her respect for Native culture and points her in the direction of the really sacred places to visit. Places only the Native Hawaiians know about and do not usually discuss with tourists. There are places like this, by the way, I'm just not telling you where they are at otherwise I may find myself getting a beating down at the shore.

When she gets back to the Mainland, she realizes she has gained super powers in the form of unbelievable strength and speed. Her embracing of Hawaiian culture has resulted in the aumakua embracing her.

**Chip:** Aumakua?

**Rex:** Hawaiian gods.

**Chip:** So, does she join the Justice League?

**Rex:** No, that's twist. Realizing the use of her powers turns her into some sort of freak show, she shuns the powers. At least in terms of what the public knows. Secretly, she uses them for good, but she never makes a spectacle of herself. In the end, she decides to give away the gift of super powers when she moves to Hawai'i where you don't need them because the aumakua take care of you. The super power there is the beauty of paradise. As she embraces her place in life, in Hawai'i, a beautiful sunset takes place right in front of her. Roll credits.

**Chip:** Do you have any celebrities attached to the project? Directors or stars?

**Rex:** No, it's just us at this point.

**Chip:** I have to say, what you have here is not bad. Your story is just different enough to note there might be something here.

**Danny:** So we're in business?

**Chip:** No, I'm going to have to pass.

**Rex:** What?

**Chip:** You guys are too green for me. I'm doing big budget successful pictures. I like remembering my roots and doing an independent from time-to-time, but you guys are too independent. You haven't made a movie before, you don't have any big name attached to it, and you're not trust fund kids bringing some cash to the deal. Basically, you're an idea. A decent one, mind you, but just an idea nonetheless. Ideas are a dime a dozen in Hollywood.

**Danny:** So where do we go from here?

**Chip:** Because I love Kiki, I've got something for you guys. Have you ever heard of Santos Ramirez?

**Rex:** No.

**Danny:** No.

**Chip:** Santos trained under Roger Corman, and he uses Roger's style, pumping out low budget movies quickly and hoping he hits on something. If one of his pictures doesn't pop for him, no worries, he's got another one coming right behind it. The guy is a bit of an eccentric, but he's actually got a pretty good system. He does everything on his compound… filming, editing, marketing, you name it. The guy is a one stop shop.

**Rex:** Does he work with any big names?

**Chip:** Absolutely. Celebrities always have vanity projects. Dream movies they want to get made but aren't right for the big studio machines. They work with Santos to simply get their movies made. He's had some minor hits. Santos is the guy for you. What you really need, though, is some celebrity to get signed on. If you can get a name attached to it, I'll bet you can get it made.

**Rex:** Have you heard of Gina Dash?

**Chip:** The singer? Sure.

**Rex:** We're trying to get her as our lead playing Kendall Beckinsail.

**Chip:** If you can make that happen Santos will want to be in business with you. Advantage Rex and Danny!

**Danny:** Would you mind calling Santos on our behalf?

**Chip:** I'll do it right now. (Picks up the phone and dials.) 'Santos, this is Chip Van der Dorr. I've got two young men in my office who work with one of my contacts in Hawai'i. They have a movie they want to pitch. It probably won't work for me, but it sounds perfect for you.' (Pauses to listen to a response). 'Okay, thanks Santos. Take care.' (Hangs up.)

**Rex:** What did he say?

**Chip:** He will see you two tomorrow morning at 9:00 a.m. I'll get you some directions.

Danny looked over at Rex knowing they are scheduled to be back in Kaua'i for work, but Rex didn't even hesitate in his response, "Perfect, we will see him then." After getting the directions to Santos' compound, the men say their goodbyes.

**Rex:** Thank you very much for your time Mr. Van der Dorr.

**Danny:** We appreciate your help.

**Chip:** All right. Tell Kiki 'aloha' for me... and be sure to tell her how helpful I was for you.

As the boys leave, Danny frantically begins inquiring what they are going to do about work, and the appointment they now have tomorrow. Rex reassures him they will figure it out. "It's pa'u hana time my friend," he says. "We'll figure everything out over some drinks."

The boys pulled into Stark Bar on Wilshire for some drinks and lunch. After being informed they didn't carry Līhue Brewing Coconut Stout, both Rex and Danny ordered Golden Road Hefeweizens, a local offering. Upon tasting their beers, they shrugged their shoulders to denote it was okay… not Līhue Brewing Coconut Stout good, but manageable in a pinch. They then began discussing their situation.

**Danny:** We're done, man. The dream is over.

**Rex:** What do you mean?

**Danny:** Where do I begin? We were told we didn't have a movie we could get produced, we have an appointment tomorrow when we are supposed to be back home working on a project, and we were called clowns and donkeys.

**Rex:** I don't see it that way.

**Danny:** You don't? The guy couldn't be any more direct. He said we were too green. We were just an idea. He is now passing us off just so he can stay in good with Kiki. He wants to act like he's helping us but he's not. You didn't see and hear that?

**Rex:** He was direct, but don't forget, he's Dutch.

**Danny:** What do you mean?

**Rex:** His last name is Van der Dorr so he's of Dutch ancestry. They are very direct people. For example, if you have someone standing in your way on a bus, you might very well say, 'Pardon me, sir, I need to squeeze through to get off of the bus.' A Dutch person would say, 'Move.' They aren't mean spirited in their approach. They are just efficient in their directness. The fact he's offering to help at all indicates he believes in us.

**Danny:** Say we do go see Santos Ramirez tomorrow…

**Rex:** We do go see Santos Ramirez tomorrow.

**Danny:** Very funny. So we go see him. Our Dutch friend told us the only way we're getting this movie made would be to get a celebrity attached. We don't have that!

**Rex:** I've got an idea. Technology levels the playing field for guys like us. I see Gina Dash is very responsive to fans on Twitter. I've got over 600 followers on Twitter. I'm kind of a big deal on there. (Pulling out his phone.) I'll send her a tweet right now. Here we go, @ginadash. See the little blue check mark?

**Danny:** Yes.

**Rex:** Well that indicates it has been verified as really being her by the good folks at Twitter. Here's a bit of trivia for you Danny Bandera, did you know the guy who invented Twitter was from St. Louis?

**Danny:** Nope.

**Rex:** Hash tag, how about that! Okay, here we go, '@ginadash I am a producer with a project I would like to speak to you about.Have 9 a.m. meeting w/Santos Ramirez Wed2pitch.Friend/DM me4info'

Tweet!

Okay, done. Now we wait. This just might work.

**Danny:** I'm sure she's going to respond to some random guy through Twitter hiring her. Why don't you just give her directions to your house? Even if we hit the lottery, and she says 'yes,' we can't even do this. We have a plane to catch. Sam Māhoe isn't going to let us off.

**Rex:** Māhoe owes us a comp day for our travel day on Monday. He said it himself. I'll call him and let him know we are taking it tomorrow.

**Danny:** I guess give it a try, it's all we've got.

**Rex (dialing phone):** Sam, this is Rex Palakiko. You know that comp day you mentioned at our Thursday meeting. (listening). The comp day for traveling to Honolulu on Monday. I'm with Danny Bandera, and we need to take that tomorrow. (listening). I know Sam. It's an important project. We'll get right on it on Thursday. (Hangs up the phone).

**Danny:** You didn't say goodbye.

**Rex:** He said fine, take it off, I am going to be there so I will see you on Thursday and hung up. I'm thinking he's busy. We're fine. I'm sure of it.

With Rex calming Danny down, they made the change to the airfare, ordered two more Golden Roads and started on some small talk.

**Rex:** If we just had more time I am sure we could really get a solid plan together. We're flying by the seat of our pants here. If we had another week here I am sure we could land someone like Tina Fey for the movie.

**Danny:** If it's so easy to get Tina Fey, why don't we just do it?

**Rex:** Easy is a relative term. It takes some navigation of the celebrity pecking order and some time. How I would see this one happening is to befriend Amy Poehler. She's so close to Tina Fey it's then an easy transition to get Tina's ear.

**Danny:** Why is Amy Poehler involved in this scenario? Why aren't you just going to Tina Fey?

**Rex:** Tina's a bigger star. Clearly you aren't saying Tina and Amy are the same level of celebrity, are you?

**Danny:** Tina is somewhat more successful, but Amy's not bad. I'm thinking while Tina may be a rung above Amy on the pecking order, the effort it would take to befriend either would be the same. To then think you could transfer this friendship to the other automatically is even more absurd than the original concept of simply becoming Amy Poehler's buddy.

Sensing Rex wasn't going to come over to his side on the Tina Fey stand-off, Danny decides to mix it up by completely changing the subject.

**Danny:** Did I ever tell you about the time our summer house flooded?

**Rex:** No, why?

**Danny:** In 1980, my parents thought it would be a good idea to buy a vacation home.

**Rex:** Sounds nice.

**Danny:** It does, until you realize they selected High Ridge, Missouri, which was like 28 minutes driveway to driveway from our house.

**Rex:** I could see the merits of a getaway so close to home. Friday night you get home from work, you get away and most of your time is spent enjoying yourself in your vacation home rather than traveling.

**Danny:** Agreed. The concept is fine, it was the practical application of what they did. They bought a place for like $3,500.

**Rex:** A house?

**Danny:** Exactly! A house. Unfortunately, they got $3,500 worth of house. We spent like a year just working in there. Cleaning, scrubbing, throwing away trash like used diapers and stuff the squatters who were living there before us left behind.

**Rex:** Once you got it done, was it nice?

**Danny:** It was better. It was right on the Big River, there was some land to spread out, but there were several shortcomings.

**Rex:** Like?

**Danny:** No air conditioning or bathrooms.

**Rex:** No bathrooms?

**Danny:** Nope. Outhouse. My dad got one of those road side construction outhouses and that was our toilet.

**Rex:** That's no vacation.

**Danny:** Especially when your home bathroom was only 28 minutes away. If I was old enough to drive, and I had to burn a mule as they say, I would have driven home. The place finally started looking good, we enjoyed some weekends there and then in 1982 the place flooded. I mean it was a wreck. Stagnant river water through the whole place.

**Rex:** Did you sell it?

**Danny:** No, my parents decided to start over, clean it up and try again. You would think my parents would be like, 'We are going to fix this place up, and it starts with the bathroom;' but they didn't. We jump in and start cleaning the interior of the house. In the meantime, the bathroom is trashed. Filled with mud, river refuse and stench. Sure enough, about an hour in, my dad is like, 'I've got to use the bathroom.' My mom is like, 'You're a man, just go outside and go behind a tree," but my dad was like 'No, I *really* have to go.'

She finally understands he has to take a dump so she says, just go stand behind the outhouse which was down by the river, far away from the house. My dad grabs a paper bag and heads out.

Now I'm twelve at the time. My only thought was, 'I have to see this,' so I tag behind him, staying far enough back he doesn't realize he's got someone tailing him. He disappears behind the outhouse. I wait like a minute and then peek around.

**Rex:** Oh no. What did you see?

**Danny:** Well, I saw my dad, standing upright, with a bag at his feet…

**Rex:** He wasn't squatting?

**Danny:** Oddly, no. These turds were coming out like a chocolate soft serve machine at Dairy Queen and hitting the side of the bag, the ground; basically anything but inside the bag. Then I'm thinking this is something which will naturally decompose. Why does he even have a bag? He then sees me and starts yelling. The funny thing was, there was three guys in a canoe, right at the river bank, watching this whole thing. Can you imagine the stories they have to tell? You know every once in a while, over a few beers they get to talking about this story to this day. Some big naked dude standing straight up straddling a paper bag with large white butt cheeks occasionally spreading apart to birth bouncing brown turds all over the ground?

**Rex:** Why are you telling me this?

**Danny:** Because we're in Los Angeles. La-La Land. The epicenter of movie stardom. We need to look around. Right now our search is like a man on a river bank pooping in a bag without even looking at the river. We're sitting in a bar drinking, and they don't even serve Līhue Brewing Coconut Stout. It's time for us to assess what we are doing here, brah.

**Rex:** You know what, you're right, let's get out of here and go find us a celebrity!

The guys squared up their tab and hit the town. Rex and Danny spent the rest of the afternoon driving to all of the celebrity hotspots they've heard about on TV: the Arclight Cinema, Chateau Marmont, The Ivy, Coldwater Canyon Park, The Grove and Beverly Hills Nail Design.

Nothing.

They saw one guy who looked like Nick Nolte. It turns out it was just some homeless guy.

Finally, as night fell, they drove to a hotel. The grabbed their bags and started heading in. Rex began whistling The Walker, "Whhh, whhh, whhh, whhh…"

Without hesitation, Danny dropped his bag and slapped Rex right across the face.

**Rex:** Are you kidding me?

**Danny:** Ghosts. Dark. Whistling.

**Rex:** That doesn't apply here. We aren't in Hawai'i.

**Danny:** Oh? That's only in Hawai'i?

**Rex:** Yes, it is.

**Danny:** My bad.

In order to make sure they arrived to Santos Ramirez's place on time, they arrived early and went to a coffee shop down the street. There they talked about their meeting this morning.

**Danny:** Same plan as the deal yesterday?

**Rex:** Yes, I'll take the lead. Look at this (taking some printed materials out of his bag): script treatments!

**Danny:** Where did you get those?

**Rex:** I wrote it last night and had the desk clerk at the hotel print me three copies while you were in the shower. Now we look professional.

**Danny:** Any news on Gina Dash?

**Rex (checking phone):** Nothing yet. Let's hold off on talking about it as long as possible in our meeting with Santos. I'm telling you I have a feeling about this. I'm feeling the pomaika'i on this one.

**Danny:** The what?

**Rex:** Good luck. I'm feeling lucky about this. I think Gina will reach out to us. It may happen when we are in the meeting, but it's going to happen. As long as I see it on Twitter, coming in from her account, I know we are good. It's going to happen.

**Danny:** Pomaika'i, baby! Hey, when I slapped you last night, why doesn't the whistling thing apply here?

**Rex:** Because, like I told you before, when we were at home, it's a local thing.

**Danny:** So by that you mean it's a Hawaiian-thing?

**Rex:** Danny, if you are going to live in Hawai'i, this is something you really need to work on.

**Danny:** What?

**Rex:** Native Hawaiian versus local.

**Danny:** Okay, I'm willing to learn, what's the difference?

**Rex:** Well, it goes like this. Things I refer to as Native Hawaiian are the traditions tied to the native people of Hawai'i. These are the customs and foods of our people. These items aren't to be mocked, changed to make them more mainstream or really used by anyone other than true Hawaiians.

**Danny:** Okay, this makes sense. What is local, then?

**Rex:** In Hawai'i we have a culture like no other place on the Earth. On the sugar plantations you had the Native Hawaiians working side-by-side with Japanese, Filipino, Chinese, Korean and German workers. These close working and living conditions meant there was a big incidence of cross-cultures occurring. The blended society of the sugar plantations had a large influence on the Hawaiian Islands. These foods and traditions from multiple cultures would be known as local.

From those outside of Hawai'i, it can be confusing. It's not uncommon for them to think of the traditions and foods from the mixed communities as being what they see as Hawaiian culture. After all, it can be found only in Hawai'i. While it is uniquely Hawaiian, the true Hawaiian culture comes from the Native Hawaiians, not the amalgamation of cultures which was fostered by the sugar plantations.

For instance foods like poke, kalua, poi, and lau-lau are traditional Hawaiian foods. Other foods like teriyaki chicken, Spam Musubi, bulgogi and lomi-lomi are often viewed as "Hawaiian cuisine," but in reality, they have either been partially or wholly influenced by individuals coming into Hawai'i. Hence the term "local" to separate what is Native Hawaiian and what is uniquely Hawaiian.

It's offensive for many Native Hawaiians to hear of something considered local to be called Hawaiian, or even worse, Native Hawaiian. I realize it is often not done out of malice, but instead ignorance, or indifference to Native Hawaiian culture, but it's hurtful nonetheless.

**Danny:** Wow, that is probably the most detailed and informative description of this I have ever heard. I mean you even used the word amalgamation. This was impressive. It makes sense. I promise to try to be as sensitive as possible to this.

**Rex:** As long as you are trying, I think people are happy about that. I think it's about time to head to see Santos.

Danny and Rex grabbed their coffees and jumped in their rental car and headed up the road to the 47-acre estate of Santos Ramirez. It now seems he is the last chance Danny and Rex have to make their movie. If this meeting doesn't go well they are just a couple of dreamers.

Fallbrook, California is known as the Avocado Capital of the World based on the large number of avocado farms in the area. Fallbrook is also home to the 47-acre all-in-one film compound of Santos Ramirez. It's situated 104 miles from Hollywood, but it has the feel of being on the other side of the world from the glamor and glitz of Tinseltown.

Throughout the 1970s, Ramirez worked for Roger Corman as a jack-of-all-trades. He would jump in and help out with whatever was needed to complete a film. His duties included, but weren't limited to, set building, camera work, editing and even some acting. After purchasing his current parcel of land in 1981, Ramirez broke off on his own and started producing his own pictures using the style of Corman. He would produce features quickly for a low budget. His money would be made through sheer volume, not necessarily big paydays from mega-hits.

Santos Ramirez has so refined his approach, it's now as equal parts Henry Ford as it is Roger Corman. For the last decade, he has shot 12 films a year with a budget of one million dollars each. Twelve million dollars for twelve films. Most small independent feature films cost more than a single Santos Ramirez film.

Ramirez's one film a month approach is a pressure packed environment pushing artists, directors and actors to the brink by keeping them moving forward towards completion of the project in order to get onto the next. They start shooting the first of the month for two weeks, edit for two weeks and release the first of the next month when Santos Ramirez and team are already shooting their next feature. All of this is accomplished with Ramirez taking a hands-on role to all of his films and a skeleton crew who support the efforts by taking on multiple roles.

The Santos Ramirez Movie Factory, as it's known, is, in fact, extremely success. The one million budget means they only need to get four million at the box office to pay for all of the distributors and break even. His business model revolves around making four million dollars back per film in order to at least break even. His bank account builds as he grows above that amount and shrinks when he falls below.

In Ramirez's world, six million is a breakout hit, eight million is a blockbuster and ten million is his stretch goal. Few go beyond ten million, but occasionally he gets into the low double digits with his box office rake. Most of his films fall in the three to six million dollar range at the box office with his biggest film to date being sixteen million dollars for a slasher film starring Michael Madsen. He also has additional revenue streams from DVD, online streaming and the occasional TV deal. Most of those additional dollars are going to be based upon the success of the film in its initial box office run.

In theory, Santos Ramirez's approach should not work. It shirks the tried-and-true studio system of the Hollywood machine. Why it works, though, lies in Ramirez himself and the work he has done making his own movies over the course of the last thirty-plus years. He gets his pictures from concept to theater. Every celebrity has a picture they want to get made. If they don't have the box office draw of the upper echelon of Hollywood elite, they likely cannot get a studio to back them.

Ramirez, on the other hand, banks on individual celebrities to get him the six million plus grosses he is seeking. He takes the leap of faith on the celebrity names to sell tickets, even if the films, or the film making approach, doesn't appear to be the quality of the movies his competitors are putting out.

It would seem Ramirez is the ultimate Hollywood outsider. He has never received any of the awards bestowed on filmmakers with much less experience than he. None of his movies have been nominated, nor has any of the stars while appearing in a Santos Ramirez film been nominated for any of the industry awards associated with excellence in filmmaking. Still, because he has worked with so many celebrities, and helped them get their dream projects produced, he is revered in Hollywood. Making a Santos Ramirez film might not have the prestige of an Academy Award, but it is a badge of honor which many celebrities speak fondly of and note it gives them the feeling they have made it in Hollywood.

Rex Palakiko and Danny Bandera are about to enter his office. They do not have name recognition, a celebrity commitment nor the cash Santos Ramirez would seek in working with a new partner. They have an idea.

Santos Ramirez has a spiral-bound notebook on his desk with hundreds of ideas. Rex and Danny have their work cut out for them if they are to convince Santos Ramirez to make *Kapu Powers*.

Driving up to Santos Ramirez's office, it looks like a dirtier and more dilapidated back stage tour at Universal Studios. There are shanty town neighborhoods dotted all over the landscape. Cars, bikes, motorcycles and other props are strewn seemingly randomly throughout the property. Additionally, several storage sheds, most of which have the doors open and apparently overstuffed with items used in Santos Ramirez's movies.

At the end of the drive is a small house, a building marked "Santos Ramirez Studios" and an old trailer with a sign that says, "Office."

They knock on the trailer door and a woman answers and lets them in. She introduces herself as Debbie, Mr. Ramirez's assistant and has Rex and Danny take a seat. The trailer is apparently divided in half with the receptionist sitting at the front of the trailer and Santos' office in the back half of the trailer behind a closed door.

It's quite different than the professional office of Chip Van der Dorr. No waterfall in the lobby, marble foyer, cubicles of busy workers and offices with a view. Rex and Danny are sitting on old kitchen chairs in a makeshift receptionist area with wood paneled walls decorated with faded movie posters from old movies Ramirez has made.

At ten after nine, a bearded man in disheveled clothes holding a giant cup of coffee emerges. "Hello," he states, "I am Santos Ramirez. Welcome to Hollywood South" as he cracks a smile.

Rex and Danny introduce themselves and follow Santos into his office as he shuts the door behind them. Santos gets the conversation going.

**Santos:** Gentlemen, a recommendation from Chip Van der Dorr… pretty impressive. What brings you to my humble office today?

**Rex:** We have a movie we think you might be interested in.

**Santos:** Really. I'm always interested in a good story.

**Rex (smiling confidently at Danny):** Great. I've got a treatment I would like you to check out.

**Santos:** A treatment?

**Rex:** You know, a brief overview of our proposed project and summary of the story?

**Santos:** This isn't Hollywood. We aren't in a class about how to pitch a movie. We are in a film studio with a guy who makes movies. Do you know an actor by the name of Johnny Depp?

**Rex & Danny (in unison, respectively):**
Sure!/Absolutely!

**Santos:** Did you know all of my movies combined last year cost less than Johnny Depp's salary for one of his movies? You know what else? My movies made more profit than Johnny Depp's last year. That's who I am. Let me show you where this so called treatment belongs (Santos tosses it in the trash with gusto). There, done. Now… let's talk movies!

**Danny:** We can do that. Rex, tell him all about it.

**Rex:** We have a superhero story for you.

**Santos:** Superhero?

**Rex:** Yes, the greatest and most unique superhero story you've ever heard.

**Santos:** Son, easy on the superlatives. You aren't going to win me over with fluff. Tell me your story.

**Rex:** I'm 100% Native Hawaiian. My heritage is rich in tradition, sacred places in our native land and oral history. Our story is about a woman from the Mainland who is able to enter this world, and she walks away with super powers when she returns home. The thing is, she shuns it. Life is a fishbowl for a superhero. She knows that. Instead of turning her life into a 24-hour newsfeed, she uses her powers discreetly.

When she finally realizes by the very nature of her using these gifts that she can't keep them a secret forever, she elects to give them up and return to Hawai'i where her powers are useless.

**Santos:** Why are they useless?

**Rex:** Because in our native land, the aumakua have the superpowers.

**Santos:** Aumakua?

**Rex:** Hawaiian gods.

**Santos:** I've never made a superhero movie. (There is an awkward pause as he waits for one of the boys to respond).

**Danny:** It could be a positive or a negative. On one hand, this is a genre you haven't explored before.

**Santos:** And on the other hand?

**Danny:** There may be a reason you haven't made a superhero movie.

**Santos:** For instance…

**Danny:** We'll, I'm just guessing here, but I would have to say it comes down to either you simply don't like superhero movies or you haven't ever gotten a good script.

**Santos:** The superhero movie is a difficult genre to film using my approach. People have expectations. Those expectations are tied to what they know from the big budget summer blockbusters typically associated with superhero movies.

I film everything here. I'm not talking about here in California, or the city of Fallbrook. I am talking all right here on my property. Did you see the woods you drove past on the way in?

**Rex and Danny (in unison):** Yes

Santos: We filmed both ***Woods Stranger*** and ***Lookout, He's Got a Knife*** completely in those woods. ***Witch in the Kitchen*** was filmed in this trailer. We'd switch up the entire interior to either look like a kitchen, a living room or a bedroom five times a day to keep up with the shoot. Vera Farmiga died right over there (pointing to the back corner) in that movie.

You didn't see it on the way in, but I have 11 acres which is a beautiful downtown. Anytown, USA. Paved streets with businesses and homes. You can shoot anything there. I even have a dedicated paved acre for highway shoots.

In the large building next to my office, we have my studio. I've got a soundstage for indoor shoots, a green screen room for special effects, an editing room, an industrial kitchen and a warehouse and distribution center for my mail order DVD business.

We put out one film a month. You know how many people it takes to run the top film producing studio, non-porn of course, in California?

**Rex:** Sixty-five.

**Danny:** No way, more like a hundred.

**Santos:** Besides me, nine. You met Debbie. She's been my assistant since I started this business. I have Sandro, who is my groundskeeper. Reggie is my set guy. He can fix or build anything. Sandro helps him out with big projects. Donnie and Lou are my camera guys, and they double up as my film editors. Rochelle runs my mail order business, is my set/costume designer and inventory control manager. She knows where every prop or costume is in this place. If you need to order something new for a movie it must be approved by her before it can be purchased. Even I don't get anything for a movie without her approval. Helps me keep on top of my budgets. Jack is my business manager. He maintains the relationships with the distributors. He's a flunked out film student, but he helps me as a second unit director when needed, as well. We call Kenny "the intern" since he literally started as an intern and technically doesn't have a job here. I mean we do pay Kenny now, but he just helps out everyone else as needed. With this small of an operation, if someone calls in sick, or takes a vacation, there's no one else to fill-in. Kenny works every job in the place. He's done everything from directing movies to pulling weeds. Mary Ann is my bookkeeper. She's also in charge of fan mail and maintaining my website and advertising. Finally, Hamburger is my executive chef. Really, he's just a line cook, but he insists on the title of executive chef. He says it's good for his résumé. I'm not sure why a guy who has been with me for twenty-five years needs an updated résumé, but we humor him by giving him the title and a white coat with his name on it.

**Rex:** You have someone named Hamburger who is your chef?

**Santos:** His last name is Halper so he got the nickname Hamburger.

**Rex:** Oh, Hamburger Halper. So he runs your craft services on your movie sets?

**Santos:** Something like that.

**Rex:** I heard the food on the sets of movies is incredible.

**Santos:** Well, I'm sure you could gain ten pounds on the set of *Ironman 27*, but like everything around here, we're a step or two below what you might see a hundred miles north. Anyway, the way I approach the movie business, you can't really shoot a superhero movie without it coming across as campy. More along the lines of that old TV show the *Greatest American Hero*. It was a decent show, it's just not what someone wants to see in the theater.

**Rex:** With all due respect, we have a different animal here.

**Santos:** In what way?

**Rex:** Our heroine has covert powers. She's trying to hide them. It could be shot in a manner which they were either obstructed or hidden from the viewer. We hide them from the audience, just like Kendall Beckinsail is trying to hide them from the world. Plus, her powers are super strength and super speed. These aren't exactly the hardest super powers to work with on film. It's not like she's flying around the globe.

**Santos:** So what exactly are you here for?

**Danny:** We want to get this film made.

**Santos:** Yes, I know that. There are many reasons, though, a filmmaker visits someone like me. Maybe they want to sell me a script, perhaps they need a place to shoot their own film, maybe they want to be involved but behind the scenes. See, there are any number of ways people like you want to engage someone like me, so, please, tell me why you are here.

**Rex:** Well, like Danny said, our priority is to get this movie made. That's the end game for us. We know the concept is solid, the script is great and audiences will love it. At the same time, we aren't trying to simply sell you a script, this film is something we want to be a part of organically from the beginning. We don't have the experience, contacts or resources to get it done on our own. Working with you and the entire team here sounds great.

**Santos:** How would you be working with us? Guys without the experience, contacts and resources seems like you might be more in the way than of assistance.

**Rex:** We respect your role as the filmmaker. Your dream, at least why you got into the business, is to bring written words to life and to find an audience for them. Our dream was to write a great story and then it get it brought to life via film. We sit here, in your office today, at the crossroad where our goals intersect. Let's now go on this journey together to fulfill both of our dreams.

Santos Ramirez bursts into laughter. He then turns to Danny and says:

**Santos:** Is this kid always like this? He's full of it, isn't he?

**Danny:** That he is. Someday, when you've got at least an hour, ask him the difference between a Native Hawaiian and a Local. If he's passionate about something it comes through, and he's pretty well spoken. Trust me, we are both passionate about working with you to get this film made.

**Rex:** Plus, we want to be here because I am the lead male role in the film.

**Santos:** Oh, you act, too?

**Rex:** Well, I never have before, but I wrote this story. The main male character, Captain Donovan, is me. I was the person who wrote the script, I envisioned myself as a I wrote his part and only one person can bring him to life onscreen, and that's me.

**Santos:** This Captain Donovan, what are his superpowers.

**Rex:** None. He's just a guy like you and me. Well, strike that. Actually he's just a guy like me, because he is me. No super powers. Just a strong name.

**Santos:** All right, let's do a reading, right now. Do you have a script here?

**Rex:** I do.

**Santos:** Okay, prove to me you are Captain Donovan.

Rex opens up two of his scripts and pulls out a page from each of a scene with Captain and Kendall. He hands Santos a copy and keeps a copy himself.

**Rex:** All right, I will be Captain Donovan and you are Kendall Beckensail. We can just pick up from the top of this page.

**Santos:** Okay. Let's do this. (In his normal speaking voice he begins). I bought our tickets to Hawai'i today.

**Rex: (joy on his face):** Great honey. I can't wait to go see Pearl Harbor, do some snorkeling and go to a luau.

**Santos:** I was thinking we could stay away from those touristy type of activities and embrace the spirit of the islands by studying the culture of the Native Hawaiians.

**Rex (inquisitively and casually):** Does this studying, as you put it, involve me with a rum-based drink in one of those half-shelled coconuts with a little umbrella popping out of the top?

**Santos:** Of course not. We can just go to a pool with a tiki bar here for the experience you are looking for. I'm talking about the real Hawaiian culture, not the caricature of the islands most people think of as Hawaiian culture.

**Rex (serious, yet charming):** Honey. Sweetie. Is it possible for one person in a party of two to embrace culture while another lies on the beach with a rum-based drink in half a coconut and a little umbrella?

**Santos:** Rex, I have to say, that wasn't half bad.

**Danny:** Rex, that was really good, man. You see, when he's passionate about something it comes through in everything he does in regard to it.

**Santos:** Gentleman, what you have here may work. I need to read the script, and I also need to know what star you have tied to this project. Nothing gets made here without someone with a fan base to sell tickets. Who is your star? Hopefully, it's someone for your lead character.

The moment of truth had arrived. It all comes down to whether or not Gina Dash responded to Rex's Twitter message. He looked down at his phone and then over to Danny. His deflated look told the story even before he gently shook his head "no" to Danny.

**Rex:** Unfortunately, we don't have anyone famous attached to the project. We envisioned Gina Dash, the singer, as being perfect. We've tried to reach out to her but haven't had any luck.

**Santos:** Well, gentlemen, I do say I have to pass at this time. Keep working on getting someone attached to it. If you make that happen, reach out to me. Maybe we can work out a deal then. Would you like to go see some filming before you go? We've got a second unit doing some scenes down at our Anytown, USA lot.

**Rex:** There isn't any chance you would still make the film?

**Santos:** I can't. I have a tested approach. I don't vary from it.

**Rex:** Stars love working with you. Don't you have someone who doesn't have a script they are pitching but just wants to be in one of your movies?

**Santos:** We get that occasionally. We use them as additional stars in movies. It's like I have an all-star cast then. Not just one recognized face.

**Danny:** If we get someone, we call you?

**Santos:** Just call Debbie.

With that, the door opened and Debbie walked in.

**Debbie:** Santos, I have a call for you.

**Santos:** Okay, these gentleman were leaving. Can you show them out?

**Rex:** Can we just drive down to your Anytown lot and see the filming before we go?

**Santos:** Sure.

**Debbie:** Santos, this call is for all three of you. This woman says it's an emergency and she needed me to interrupt this meeting.

Rex and Danny look at each other knowing exactly who it is.

**Rex:** Unbelievable! Gina Dash comes through at the eleventh hour!

**Debbie:** Gina Dash? The singer? No, it's not Gina Dash. Do you know her? I'm a big fan.

**Danny:** Not Gina Dash? Who is it, then?

**Debbie:** I have no idea. Some woman named Cas.

Rex and Danny look at each other inquisitively. Both are shrugging their shoulders in the international gesture of "I don't know."

**Santos:** Put her through.

The phone rings and Santos puts her on speaker.

**Santos:** Hello, this is Santos Ramirez. I have you on speaker phone with Rex and Danny.

**Cas:** Hey guys.

**Rex:** Hey, Cas.

**Danny:** Hello, Cas.

**Rex:** Cas, what's going on here, why are you calling us and more importantly how did you know where to find us?

**Cas:** Rex, I saw your post on Twitter.

**Santos:** Young lady, do we have a reason for this call beyond saying hello to a couple of friends?

**Cas:** Absolutely. I saw Rex was really desperate to get Gina Dash for the meeting so I reached out to an old friend.

**Rex:** So you do know Gina Dash?

**Cas:** Better than that. I've got someone on the line I want to introduce you to.

**Cas' Friend:** Hello, gentlemen.

Danny stood up out of his chair as his eyes got as big as saucers.

**Danny:** Oh my god, are you kidding me. That's Bob Weir. Bob Weir of the Grateful Dead. RatDog. That is the real Bob Weir. I would know that voice anywhere.

**Bob Weir:** It is the Bob Weir.

Santos Ramirez moved closer to the phone. In doing so, he accidentally hit his cup and spilled his coffee all over his desk. Ignoring it, he continued talking.

**Santos:** Mr. Weir, I am a big fan. I saw you at Fillmore East in 1970.

**Danny:** What?

With that Danny tears off his shirt and turns around exposing his back with the Fillmore East tattoo on it to Santos Ramirez.

**Rex:** Everyone. Hold on. I don't know what's going on here. We have a coffee spill. A living legend on the phone. A friend from Hawai'i is calling us during a business meeting. I have some idiot not wearing a shirt during said business meeting. I really have no idea what's happening right now.

**Cas:** Bob, tell them.

**Bob Weir:** I've been friends with Cas for many years. I haven't heard much from her since she moved to Hawai'i, but she reached to me out of the blue yesterday. She told me what you guys were doing and wondered if I knew Gina Dash. Get this, I had Gina Dash opening for me on my last RatDog tour. She's a really close friend. She's out finishing up a tour right now, so it was difficult to reach her. I finally did speak to her just a few moments ago. She's in for your project, if you still want her.

**Rex:** Are you kidding? Of course, we do.

**Santos:** I have to tell you, with Gina Dash on, we can do this project. In fact, my movie set for next month can be pushed back. Would Gina be available as early as the first of next month?

**Bob Weir:** She said she would. Her tour finishes up next week.

**Santos:** Guys, if we can lock in Gina, we start filming next month.

**Bob Weir:** Cas and I were talking. She's been such a good friend I want to be a part of this, too. Santos, if there is a song from my catalog you want to use for the film, let me know. I know you work on a slim budget. No charge. Just get it in the credits… and list Cas Schwabe in there, too.

**Santos:** You got it my friend. I thank you for this, Mr. Weir.

**Bob Weir:** Just Bob is fine. Okay, I've got to run now. Keep me updated with your project.

**Rex:** Cas, keep on the line when Bob hangs up.

**Cas:** Okay.

Everyone said goodbye to Bob, he hung up and the conversation continued.

**Santos:** Cas, how do you know Bob Weir?

**Cas:** I used to follow the Grateful Dead. I did for many years. I became friends with Bob and the rest of the band over time. You know Grateful Dead fans, we are all about community.

Rex looked knowingly over at Danny.

**Danny:** You never mentioned you knew anyone from the Grateful Dead.

**Cas:** I guess we never spoke about it. You were always asking me about my movie star friends from my days on the set or my music buddies from my work as a personal chef. Bob is an old friend. Actually, more like family than a friend.

**Danny:** You knew I liked the Grateful Dead. The tattoos. The hat you had Maxine make me.

**Cas:** Don't you think I would have come across as braggadocios if I would have been like, oh you're a fan, well, I'm their friend?

**Danny:** Okay, I see what you are saying.

**Rex:** Cas, you said you would never ask one of your celebrity friends anything like how to help us out by being in a movie. Why did you ask Bob?

**Cas:** Like I said, Bob's family. It wasn't going to hurt our relationship to ask. I had no idea he had the connection, but I saw the desperate tweet you made and thought I would try to help out.

**Rex:** Well, you made it at the last minute.

**Cas:** The last minute? Hey, I was working my butt off for you guys. I had to track down Bob. There's the time difference. We then had to try to reach Gina, and I figured this all needed to be done in time for your movie. Bob agreed to do it, but it was hard reaching Gina since she's in Europe right now.

**Rex:** Trust me, we couldn't be any happier with you than we are right now. You rock!

**Santos:** Do you want a part in the movie Ms. Cas?

**Cas:** No, I'm pretty busy with my business here on Kaua'i. I can't afford the time to be in a movie.

**Rex:** How about if you had Maxine Graham work on some crew hats for the set? We need 10 for the staff here, plus ones for myself and Danny. My treat for those!

**Cas:** I think that can be arranged, so long as we get my Akamai Juice logo on there too.

**Rex:** Absolutely. Take care Cas.

**Danny:** Bye Cas!

**Santos:** Goodbye.

**Cas:** See you, everyone!

**Santos:** Okay, I've got some paperwork for you guys. Everything I do is standard in terms of pay with me. It doesn't matter who you are. When we made the movie *A Stranger in the Alps*, John Goodman signed on with me at $1,500 a week to act the same week he signed an eight million dollar deal to star in a studio-backed movie. Of course, most of his money with me was tied to the backend based on movie performance. We did pretty good with that one so John made a profit in the end. Nothing near his eight million dollar studio payday, but this was a movie he's always wanted to make, and he was able to say he not only made it, he made money off of it.

**Danny:** John Goodman, really? He's from St. Louis. Was he good to work with?

**Santos:** The guy was awesome. Like everything, we shot everything here. You probably saw those shacks on the drive in.

**Danny:** Yes.

**Santos:** That was the Alpine village. The woods were the mountains in the Alps. Of course, we're in Southern California. Not exactly the Alps. Luckily, my brother worked for a food broker. He had four pallets of mashed potato flakes he had to pick up which were out of date. We used them to create the snow. We had to open every box. Of course, that was all of the snow we had. Four pallets. It sounds like a lot, but we you are talking snow for multiple days of filming covering a whole village it's not that much. Since we didn't have access to anymore I had to have my crew picking this stuff up and moving it when we switch from the village to the woods. Goodman was rolling around in it for much of the movie. By the end, that was some pretty dirty potato flake snow. It should be noted, every day on the set, Hamburger served mashed potatoes. I swear he was scooping up some of our snow and serving it to the crew. He denied it, but I know better.

**Danny:** So how does the pay work?

**Santos:** It's all here in this contract. You both receive a lump sum split for writing, my standard on-set consultant fees, plus Rex will get extra for acting. Then you get backend revenue once we surpass four million in sales.

**Danny:** Actually, just Rex wrote it.

**Rex:** It doesn't matter, Santos. Just take whatever money you are paying us individually, lump it together and divide it in half. We are a team on the whole thing.

**Santos:** Great. I will have Debbie get all of this together for you. Other than the Kendall and Captain roles I will cast the rest. We start filming on the first of next month. All of this is contingent on Gina Dash signing on as Kendall Beckinsail.

**Danny:** You don't even need to read the whole script?

**Santos:** I will. What I saw looked good. I like the concept. Most of all, I like Gina Dash and a soundtrack featuring Bob Weir. I can fix the rest if need be.

**Rex:** We have a deal!

**Santos:** Great guys. This is very exciting.

**Danny (opening his briefcase):** Santos, I have a gift for you. It's two bottles of Maull's Barbecue Sauce.

**Santos:** Why are you giving me this?

**Danny:** In Hawai'i we would never show up, asking for a favor without bringing a gift. We look forward to working with you on the movie so I brought you a gift.

**Santos:** So you bring me Maull's Barbecue Sauce?

**Danny:** Traditions say it must be a gift with meaning. I'm from St. Louis originally. Maull's is a St. Louis-based company. Hence the special gift for you.

**Santos:** Can't you just buy that at Ralph's?

**Danny:** Actually that's where I picked it up. There was a Ralph's right next to our hotel.

**Santos:** Um, thanks, I guess.

Everyone shook hands and Santos led Rex and Danny out of his office back to Debbie to get busy with the paperwork. (Santos handed Debbie the barbecue sauce and instructed her to "Give it to Hamburger" prior to heading back to his office to answer some calls.)

After signing all of their documents, Santos took Rex and Danny for a short trip across the property to see his team in action. After some time view Santos' latest picture getting made, Rex and Danny headed for the airport. Their dream was about to come true, yet, seemingly, there were still a few nightmares awaiting them ahead. Not the least of which was, what were they going to do about their jobs back in Kaua'i?

As soon as they were out of sight from Santos Ramirez, Danny and Rex went crazy in the car: yelling, high fiving, fist pumps, fist bumps and general mayhem. In only a few short days they went from a couple of guys having a few coconut stouts at Kintaro's to movie producers on a Hollywood film. When the celebration finally calmed, they began to discuss the specifics of what they were about to embark on during their drive to the airport.

**Rex:** I say we go back to Kaua'i, report to Ha'ena State Park and let Sam know we are going to need a leave of absence.

**Danny:** How long do we need?

**Rex:** I'm thinking two months. We need to cover film production, editing...

**Danny:** Two months? We aren't the ones editing.

**Rex:** Santos may need us to see a rough cut. Then we have the film opening and perhaps a press tour. Two months should cover it. Who knows, if it's a big success we probably will never go back. We're in the movie business now.

**Danny:** Hey, do you see that Chevy Spark?

**Rex:** Yeah, why?

**Danny:** Isn't that a horrible color of green?

**Rex:** It's a tad bright.

**Danny:** It's called lime. When I went to buy my Elantra, I also looked at the Spark. When you used to buy a car, it was like there may have been shades, but you were buying colors like red, black and blue. When you look at the colors of a Spark it sounded like you were at the grocery store: lime, salsa, lemonade and grape.

**Rex:** Danny! Focus! We're talking about our new movie careers.

**Danny:** Rex, you do know when we have these two months off, we aren't getting paid.

**Rex:** We'll just have to live off of credit cards until our paychecks start rolling in from Santos.

**Danny:** Rex, what if we end up millionaires. What would you buy?

**Rex:** I'm not sure. I don't actually think I need anything. Maybe something for my mom and brother.

**Danny:** I'm buying Kintaro's.

**Rex:** You don't know anything about running a bar and restaurant.

**Danny:** Hey, I've spent a lot of time observing the operation from a bar stool. I could run that place.

**Rex:** It's not even for sale.

**Danny:** Everything is for sale. You just need movie money to be able to afford it.

**Rex:** All right, here's the airport. Help me find the rental car facility.

Rex and Danny pulled into LAX, dropped off their car and headed to check-in. They had a long flight ahead of them and an interesting day on tap for tomorrow with Sam Māhoe.

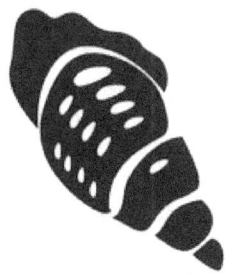

After a long day of traveling, Danny and Rex barely got home when they had to turn around and head to work. They pulled into Ha'ena State Park at the same time on Thursday morning. Sam Māhoe was already onsite waiting for them.

The plan they had discussed on the plane was to get started on the job and then talk to Sam about the leave of absence at lunch. They had decided it would have a much more casual feel over a meal versus just throwing it out there the first thing in the morning. They weren't sure what he was going to be like in terms of mood in the a.m. but felt like he would calm down by lunch if he was angry. They had even practiced their speech, playing off of one another to deliver their request with a unified front.

As soon as they were out of their cars, Sam Māhoe began talking.

**Sam:** You guys can't do to me what you did yesterday ever again. Time off is your time. I don't care what you do, but you have to give me more notice than what you did yesterday. I had volunteers lined up to help with the clean-up. I had to come out here and spend the whole day providing instructions and guidance. This is what I hired you two for. I'm not on you about taking the time off, it's just about the notice.

**Rex:** Sam, we're going to be taking a two month leave of absence.

Danny's eyes got as big as saucers. This wasn't the plan they discussed. This wasn't the speech they had practiced with each taking strategic roles in delivery.

**Sam:** Aiâ! What, are you kidding me here? This is a joke, right?

**Rex:** No Sam, we are going to help out the next two weeks and then we are going to need to be off for about two months.

**Sam:** Why?

**Rex:** We were in California yesterday, getting a movie deal with a big time Hollywood producer. Well, actually he's a big time Fallbrook, California producer, but that doesn't sound as good.

**Sam:** Shut it. Are you seriously telling me you want a leave of absence for two months to go shoot a movie?

**Rex:** We are.

**Sam:** We? I haven't heard from you, Bandera. Is this what you want to do as well?

**Danny:** Yes sir. Um, it's a really good opportunity. Like a once in a lifetime event. We'll go shoot the movie, and then we are right back here, working in the Parks Department.

**Sam:** No you're not. You two are fired. Immediately. Get out of here.

**Rex:** Sam, be reasonable.

**Sam:** You don't have to leave, but this park is closed today. If you stick around, you can join the volunteers. Effective immediately you are no longer employees of the State of Hawai'i.

**Danny:** Sam…

**Sam:** Get out now, or take off those uniform shirts, put on a t-shirt and grab a trash bag and get cleaning up as a volunteer.

Stunned, Danny and Rex turned and headed back towards their cars. As soon as they were out of earshot of Sam Māhoe they began speaking about what had just transpired.

**Danny:** Are you kidding me, right now?

**Rex:** Sam's being unreasonable.

**Danny:** You weren't supposed to say anything until lunch time. Remember, we had the plan to let him cool off. It's like we had Kilauea erupting over there.

**Rex:** Well, he had that whole speech going about you gotta give me notice, your time is your time but you gotta give me notice. I thought this was as good of a time as any to discuss our situation. I wanted to give him as much notice as possible.

**Danny:** Hey, he's looking over here. Let's go to Hanalei Coffee Roasters. We can grab a cup and gather our thoughts.

**Rex:** Sounds good, I will see you there.

After a short drive to Hanalei, the boys each grabbed a Molokai Drip Coffee and sat down to try to figure out what just happened, and what they were doing next.

**Rex:** I still can't believe Māhoe just fired us like that.

**Danny:** Well, he was angry about us leaving him hanging yesterday, and the first thing we do is ask him for a two month leave of absence. Not smart.

**Rex:** I'm telling you this would have happened no matter when we brought it up.

**Danny:** Maybe so, but we had a plan. We crafted it together. We had a unified front. If we are going to make it in the movie business, no more lone wolfin'. We develop a plan, and we stick to it.

**Rex:** You're right, you are right. We did work on what we were going to say. Even if it would have failed, which I'm telling you it would have, it would have been what we put together. I was wrong for just throwing this thing out there myself, and I'm sorry. We are a team.

**Danny:** It's cool. Maybe we've been given a gift here. Maybe this allows us to focus on making the best movie ever made, and this is our dream, our destiny.

**Rex:** Yeah, we don't need to be landscapers anymore. We are filmmakers.

**Danny:** Living the life of a filmmaker has to be one of God's greatest gifts.

**Rex:** What do you mean?

**Danny:** After childbirth, bourbon, accidental nudity, Kate Upton and Jennifer Lawrence, working as a filmmaker is probably the next one of God's greatest gifts to mankind.

**Rex:** Accidental nudity?

**Danny:** Yeah, accidental nudity is a top-fiver, for sure.

**Rex:** I don't know what it is. I mean I know what the words separately mean, but it's like you put them together and they still kinda make sense, but your speaking of the joining of them like it's a miracle or something.

**Danny:** It kind of is. Accidental nudity is exactly what it sounds like. It's nudity which happens accidentally.

**Rex:** Why is nudity, which is happening accidentally, so great?

**Danny:** Because, nudity itself is a miracle. I mean we sit there and think about naked women all day long. We're guys. We probably shouldn't do this. Certainly it's not politically correct. It's probably wrong to even whisper about it in this coffee shop. Yet it's the reality. That barista who made my coffee…

Rex turns around and looks.

**Danny:** Well, as she handed me the cup I pictured her nude handing me my Molokai Drip. It's just how it is. Now I'm not proud of that. Life shouldn't be that way. She's not encouraging me to undress her with my eyes, but it happens.

**Rex:** So accidental nudity is something like you are in a coffee shop, some woman suddenly strikes you as attractive, you then picture her sans knickers?

**Danny:** Sans knickers? Is this the Roarin' 20s?

**Rex:** You know what I mean.

**Danny:** Actually, I'm not sure I completely do, but I am getting the gist of it. The answer is, no, accidental nudity is not picturing someone nude, it's an actual event. Seeing someone naked. It has to be man seeing woman, or woman seeing man, or same sex seeing same sex if that's what they are into. This isn't sitting in the gym on a bench and some sausage walks by. That may be totally accidental, and nudity, but that's just gross.

What I'm talking about is you happen to be just going about your life, and nudity occurs. I would strike out any professional like doctor/patient relationships, negative occurrences like someone is injured or a situation where you know there will be nudity involved like going to a strip club. I'm talking about random occurrences like where you are at the pool, and someone goes down the sliding board and a booby pops out the side or the door on a dressing room malfunctions, and you happen to walk in on a babe changing.

**Rex:** Is there a crime involved here? Because it kind of sounds like something's wrong here.

**Danny:** No, that's the point. You aren't seeking it out, you aren't doing anything to make this happen. Magically, it just happens.

**Rex:** And this has happened to you?

**Danny:** Oh yeah, tons of times.

**Rex:** For example…

**Danny:** For example, back when I was married, we had a dog. I was out walking it and stumbled over a curb. I dropped the leash and the dog took off. He thought it was a game. He ended up running into a neighbor's backyard. As I'm running through the yard I look back at the house because I'm worried someone may hear me in the yard and think it's a burglar. As I look back, there is Candy Propokovicz, my next door neighbor, releasing the hounds as she drops her bra.

**Rex:** So there is a crime here. You are a peeping tom.

**Danny:** No, a peeping tom would be someone actively seeking out nudity by illegally looking in windows. I was just a guy chasing a dog. I never looked in those windows again, nor any other one, but for that brief moment, I happened to benefit from some accidental nudity.

**Rex:** So there are other stories.

**Danny:** Oh sure, tons. You don't have any?

**Rex:** Not one. I mean I haven't seen a single armadillo, never a bajingo. Heck, not even a nip slip. Not accidentally at least. I mean I like nudity. Yes, I'd even like to see more of it. So tell me, how do you go about it?

**Danny:** Well, that's the key, it needs to come to you. It's accidental after all. I would say you could best be open to this natural phenomenon by keeping your eyes open. Being aware of your surroundings. Nudity is out there, you just have to be aware of it.

**Rex:** Oh great nudity mentor, if there was one tip you had for success, what would it be?

**Danny:** I would say there are a lot of three-way mirrors in accidental nudity. That's the one takeaway you should gather from this.

**Rex:** What do you mean… three way mirrors?

**Danny:** Well, I've had several mirror accidental nudity events in my life but let me tell you about this dandy little one I had, again, back when I was married.

**Rex:** The married thing is the center of your stories.

**Danny:** Well, it's just happenstance for these examples, but I have to tell you, accidental nudity can help a marriage, I would encourage couples to keep things exciting by welcoming accidental nudity whenever it happens. Anyway, we were on this couples vacation. We were with my old friend Eric and his wife. We were planning on going to the Grand Canyon the next day. We realized my wife had Eric's phone in her purse since his wife Deena hadn't been carrying one. I thought they might want it to check-in back home. Plus, we hadn't really worked out the details: when we were leaving, what we were bringing, were we eating breakfast at the hotel or on the way there, that sort of thing.

Anyway, I thought a quick face-to-face meeting could result in me returning the phone and finding out exactly what the plan the next day was, so I knocked on their door. Eric answered. Right behind him was a mirror, which caught the reflection of another mirror across the room which in-turn provided a glimpse into the bathroom mirror where Deena was apparently standing naked.

**Rex:** So you saw your buddy's wife nude?

**Danny:** Well, I mean totally by accident, but yes, I saw Deena nude. Completely nude. Completely by accident. The very definition of accidental nudity. (He looks smugly at Rex as he punctuates his point with a Price is Right Model hand flip as he says, "accidental nudity.")

**Rex:** Was she hot?

**Danny:** Not really.

**Rex:** So why did you look?

**Danny:** She was nude.

**Rex:** Oh yeah, right. So has the tables ever been turned? Have you been the victim of accidental nudity yourself?

**Danny:** Not really.

**Rex:** It doesn't seem like there is a grey area here. Either you have been or you haven't.

**Danny:** Well, I've never actually been nude out in public, but I had a pretty bad underwear incident once. I was sent to this conference in Orlando. We got to stay in a Disney resort. My wife was helping me out by packing my bag, and she noted my workout shorts were getting thin as she put it them in my suitcase. I just ignored her thinking they probably weren't as bad as she was saying. Perhaps, if necessary, I would look into getting some new shorts when I returned home.

I get to the hotel in Orlando, and the lobby was a zoo. There are people everywhere and, of course, it was crawling with kids. I mean it's a Disney hotel, I guess it is to be expected. Once I got checked in, I decided to get a solid workout in and then rest a while before heading out for dinner. When I got to the workout room, I was pleased to see the recumbent bike was open so I climbed aboard and started pedaling. I hadn't been working out a lot, so making it through the workout was a struggle. I'm shifting around and just a lot more uncomfortable trying to keep a pace for 30 minutes than I typically am when I'm working out a lot more regularly. Ultimately, I powered my way through with sheer will and completed the workout. I decide to award myself with a Diet Pepsi since it had been such a tough time on the bike.

As I strolled through the crowded lobby on the way to the gift shop I kind of felt like people were staring at me. Of course, I'm a fat guy in workout clothes, sweating profusely, so I'm assuming people are thinking 'fat, sweaty guy in a nice hotel.' I make my way in to the gift shop. Bummer, they are a Coke shop. Not a Diet Pepsi in sight. I did remember seeing a Pepsi in the soda machine by my room, so I head back through the lobby to the elevators. I ride up with like 6 other people. Nobody said a word, but I had this weird sensation of feeling their eyes staring at me. Again, I just wrote it off as feeling weird about being in workout attire while they were either in business clothes or cabana wear.

I get off the elevator put my cash in to the machine and select Diet Pepsi. To my dismay, a bottled water drops out. This does me no good. I can get a drink of water in my room. Plus, it just cost me two bills. I'm not standing for dropping two bucks on a water I don't even want so I marched back down to the lobby. The check-in line doesn't look like it's moved since I got to the hotel but I jump in line and stand there with the rest of the cattle… again. Remember, I've got two bucks on the line here. I'm not walking away from the cash, plus it's a matter of principle at this point.

After about 20 minutes, I finally get my turn, they give me the two bucks and tell me to just go ahead and keep the water, as well. Maybe things are looking up for me, I think. I head back up the elevator towards my room. On the elevator I hear a mom tell her young son, 'shhhhh.' At this point I am like, what, has no one ever seen a guy in workout clothes? Yeah, I'm fat… I get it.

I get off the elevator and see the Pepsi machine again. The last time I knew I had selected Diet Pepsi but the machine just dispensed me the wrong beverage. What if they just stocked a lone out-of-place water in the wrong slot? A random occurrence. Perhaps I could still get Diet Pepsi. I put the two dollars in the clerk had just refunded me, make my selection of Diet Pepsi…

(singing "fail" music) wha, wha…whaaaaaaa.

Water.

Again.

Oh well. I'm not standing in line back down in the lobby, I'm just drinking the water this time. I open up my room door and as soon as I walk in, I catch a glimpse of myself in the mirror. Oh no. The whole back of my pants had just completely disintegrated. I guess all of the shifting around on the bike wore out those thinning workout shorts. I basically just walked through the lobby, the gift store, up the elevators and even stood in a snaking line in the lobby in a pair of assless chaps.

**Rex:** Aren't all chaps assless?

**Danny:** Rex, please. How had I not felt a breeze or the shreds of material slapping against the back of my creamy thighs? I think about it to this day. Sometimes life leaves you with questions without providing you the answers.

**Rex:** Oh my god, you are killing me, man. That is hilarious. Creamy thighs! (laughing)

**Danny:** Speaking of hotels, I bet hotel maids see a lot of accidental nudity. Like if the President of the United States was going to appoint someone to the Accidental Nudity Commission, it would have to be a hotel maid. Ladies and gentleman, esteemed colleagues, members of the press, I present to you Rosie from the Fairfield Inn who will now serve as our Accidental Nudity Czar. This phenomenon must stop, and Rosie will lead us on this crusade.

**Rex:** Man, I feel a lot better about what happened this morning. Maybe you were right when you said the situation of getting fired was actually a gift. We can go into this project with a clear mind and focus solely on making the best movie we can.

**Danny:** You are probably right. Let's get our plan together.

Rex and Danny spent the rest of the day working on their plan and making arrangements to move to California for the filming of their movie.

They now had everything riding on this picture.

Being cast in **Kapu Powers** represents a huge break in Gina Dash's career. Her only other film work to date had been a small part in a Reese Witherspoon movie and a larger role in an independent release. Thus far, she had never been the lead actress in any of her work. With her tour just finishing up, and Santos Ramirez style of working so quickly, she is going to be able to shoot a lead role without distracting from her primary career as the front woman of Gina Dash and the Cha-Chas, a rock-and-roll band prone to long jam sets.

The reason this movie is such an opportunity for Gina Dash lies in the fact that even while Santos Ramirez's films typically don't find a large audience amongst the general population, one group that is watching is the Hollywood machine. Directors and producers for all of the major studios comb through Ramirez's films to find undervalued talent for their own films. You might not win awards, or make a lot of money starring in a Ramirez piece, but is pretty obvious the rewards extend well beyond what comes directly from his films.

Two actors and one actress won Oscars in their next movies after their Ramirez parts. This is work these three likely wouldn't have gotten without being featured in their respective Santos Ramirez films.

Gina Dash doesn't have visions of Oscars in her near future, but she does see the potential in the movie business. There is something special about being part of a film which grabs the attention of the public. There is a level of becoming part of popular culture which rivals her success as the lead singer in a popular rock-and-roll band, yet is very different. Having found so much success as a singer, Gina wants to push herself to see if it's possible to also find there is a similar future for her in the movies.

Long before filming began Gina knew the experience of a Santos Ramirez film would be very different than her other two movies. First off, there is the experience of living on the set. Ramirez has a group of trailers on his property which not only serve as changing and resting rooms for the stars of the film, as well as the crew, they actually stay in them while shooting. This gives Ramirez the ability to work late into the night and start again early in the morning without the distractions of the outside world interfering with his cast and crew.

Secondly is the preparation and controlling nature of Ramirez. Last week she received a pack which contained copies of the storyboards Ramirez drew up based on the script Rex wrote. The storyboards are numbered, not based on the continuity of the script, but instead, to reflect the order which they will be shot. Ramirez literally has every shot lined out with a plan for filming thirteen days. He leaves one day as open in case of any production delays. He then has the wiggle room of a single day in case outside factors cause a work stoppage. If nothing goes wrong, the plan is for them to shoot thirteen days straight and complete filming a day early.

Her packet also contained minute details, all the way up to what time to arrive at the compound on day one, who to ask for upon arrival and what will be served for lunch. (Chicken fajitas on day one, for instance.) Day one will begin with all stars checking-in, getting settled in their trailers and changing into their first shoot outfits to begin filming at 9:00 a.m.

The first scene involves Gina and Rex's characters kissing for the first time in a flashback of their first date. Ramirez noted he liked for first kiss scenes to be shot early prior to the stars getting to know each other better as filming went on. Gina also noticed she was the only one with acting credits other than Iolana Keahi, who would be playing Kakalina, the woman whom she meets and befriends on the trip and then takes her to the sacred spots in Hawai'i.

While she didn't recognize Iolana by name, when she searched her name on the internet, her face looked familiar. It turns out she has a long list of credits, mostly in cameos playing a friend of another star in TV shows and movies or as a guest star in parts requiring a person from Hawai'i.

Even though she was a half hour early at 6:30 a.m., Gina decided to still check-in to Santos Ramirez Studios. She was greeted at the gate by a man in a work shirt with a patch over his left pocket which read, "Sandro." As instructed in her packet, she asked for Jack.

Sandro pointed in the right direction to find the area where all of the trailers were located. She stepped out of the car to meet a man waiting for her who immediately identified himself as Jack.

**Jack:** I recognize you. You are Gina Dash.

**Gina:** I am. Nice to meet you Jack.

**Jack:** I'm a big fan. Love your work. The song you did with Bob Weir, *Weir-Dash-It*; that was awesome.

**Gina:** Thanks, Jack. Bob is an incredible musician and even better person. I am honored to meet him, much less to be able to actually work with him. Sometimes I still can't believe it really happened.

**Jack:** All right, well, we are really enthused about having you here. This is home-sweet-home for the next two weeks. We have you set-up right over there (pointing behind Gina) in our star section. Santos has two big trailers for the leads in his movies. The rest of us are in the smaller trailers in the cast and crew village down the hill. You are staying in the one on the right, and Rex will be in the one on the left. They are clean, and everything you need is in them, including your first outfit. Rochelle, our costumer designer has your first outfit set-up in the closet. She said to tell you she will be by around 8:00 a.m. to do your hair. I'll get out of your way and let you get settled in. The others should be showing up soon.

**Gina:** Great, I do have one question.

**Jack:** Do you need help with your luggage?

**Gina:** No, I can handle it. I do need to know which trailer am I in?

**Jack:** Sorry, I thought I said that. The one on the right.

**Gina:** You did say that. Which right?

**Jack:** Pardon?

**Gina:** Which right, mine or yours? I was facing you and you were facing both me and the trailers. Your right was different than mine.

**Jack:** Yours, of course. Why would I say mine?

**Gina:** Well, I can't speak for you, but I think a lot of people speak for themselves in similar circumstances. When they say right, they mean their right. I think you try to offset that by either saying "my right or your right" or by combining a phrase like "on the right" with a pointed direction.

**Jack:** I'm sorry we don't have the fancy accommodations you are used to on big Hollywood sets here, but I think you will find our trailers more than adequate.

**Gina:** I am sure they are, I wasn't really speaking about the quality of your accommodations, though.

**Jack:** Okay. Look over there. That trailer on both of our lefts, the one that used to be on your right is your trailer.

**Gina:** Got it. I will go get ready.

**Jack:** Okay, nice to meet you Gina, looking forward to working with you (as he mumbled "Hollywood" and shook his head in disbelief at their exchange).

Over the course of the next 45 minutes, the trailer area was a hotbed of activity. Iolana Keahi and the rest of the cast and the crew arrived, checked-in and proceeded to their trailers.

At 7:15 a.m. Rex and Danny pulled onto the property and were sent back to the trailer area by Sandro. Like the rest, they pulled up to meet Jack for instructions.

**Jack:** All right, looks like we have Rex Palakiko and Danny Bandera here, right?

**Rex:** That is correct.

**Jack:** Rex, we have you right over here in the trailer on the left. Rex is in the star section along with Gina Dash who is in the other trailer and Danny, we have you with the rest of the cast and crew down the hill. Your trailer is marked #5.

**Rex:** Wow, so Gina Dash is here already?

**Jack:** She is. She checked-in about 6:30.

**Rex:** How is she?

**Jack:** Well, she's beautiful, that's for sure. A little bit of the Hollywood type. You know how these stars are. They are a little entitled… a little better than the rest of us.

**Rex:** I'm surprised by that. She seems pretty grounded when you see her interviewed. I hope she's good to work with.

**Jack:** Okay, you guys need to get going. Rex, you're your outfit for the first shots of the day is hanging in your trailer. Rochelle will be by to do your hair around 8:00.

**Rex:** Sounds good, thanks, Jack.

**Danny:** Yes, thanks, Jack.

Rex and Danny grabbed their bags and headed to their respective trailer. Rex climbed the steps of his and opened the door. Standing right in the middle of the room was someone he immediately recognized: Gina Dash. Awkward under any circumstance, this was particularly shocking because she was topless. She screamed, Rex screamed and then slammed the door shut, apologizing profusely saying it was an accident, Jack had told him to come into the wrong trailer.

Funny, Danny never mentioned the screaming, the panic and the shame associated with accidental nudity. Gina quickly threw on a shirt and came out onto the porch to properly meet Rex.

**Gina:** Well, you must be Rex.

**Rex:** I am. I am. I'm also really sorry about this whole thing.

**Gina:** Did that guy Jack really tell you the wrong trailer?

**Rex:** Well, he said the one on the left. I guess he meant my left. I assumed he meant his left. Anyway, is this trailer actually yours?

**Gina:** Yes it is.

**Rex:** Again, I'm sorry. I'm going to go get ready.

**Gina:** Rex, it's no big deal. We're artists. Our bodies are the canvasses in which we deliver our medium as actors. We shouldn't be ashamed.

**Rex:** I am in complete agreement. You have nothing to be ashamed about. Wow!

**Gina (laughing):** Thanks, Rex. I mean you startled me by walking in so suddenly, but being seen nude really doesn't bother me. I'm a musician. Music is all about the outfit changes.

Sure, the songs are important, but so are those outfit changes. I do a minimum of five per show. Half of the crew not only sees me nude backstage they are helping me get dressed because I have to do it so quickly. At first I was modest, then you get to the point, of like, 'Hey you over there in the green, grab that roll and tape up my chi-chis so I look good in this chiffon dress.'

**Rex:** Katy Perry does a lot of outfit changes.

**Gina:** Yeah, she's great, isn't she?

**Rex:** She sure is. I better get out of your way. It was nice meeting them… I mean, um, I mean it was nice meeting YOU.

**Gina (laughing):** Yeah Rex. It was nice meeting you, too. See you in a little bit.

Laughing about his first experience with accidental nudity, Rex tried to get it together as he strolled over to his trailer to get ready for his big day.

As Rex and Danny met up outside of Rex's trailer, they were approached by Jack with a young woman.

**Jack:** Hey guys, this is Stella. She says she is working here with you.

**Danny:** Oh, Stella Davis, Kiki's daughter.

**Stella:** Yep, that's me.

**Danny:** Yeah, Jack, we know her.

**Jack:** Okay guys, I'll let you go. (Turns and leaves).

**Rex:** So Stella, you are interested in the movie business?

**Stella:** Yes, I am attending UCLA studying film. I hope to be a director. I've got my first piece. It's called *The Legend of Bear Island*, and it is a story I wrote about two young boys who go to a mysterious island and end up being confronted by the spirits there. I want to try to get that made.

**Danny:** Well, working with Santos should be an exciting opportunity.

**Stella:** Absolutely. This is a chance to work with a legend in the industry. This is probably going to be better for my career than my four years of school!

**Rex:** All right, there's Santos over there. Let Danny and I go talk to him to find out what he needs you to do here.

**Stella:** Sounds good.

Danny and Rex head over to talk to Santos, knowing they haven't yet even broached the subject of Stella working on the set. They realize he's so regimented and controlling, he's probably not good with surprises, but they quickly hatch a plan as they walk over to him.

**Rex:** Hey, Santos.

**Santos:** Rex. Danny. You guys ready to make a movie?

**Danny & Rex (in unison):** Yes/Absolutely.

**Rex:** We've got a question for you. That woman over there. (Santos looks over to his left at Stella.) She's the daughter of the woman who got us our meeting with Chip Van der Dorr, which then led to our meeting with you. Her name is Stella, and she is a senior at UCLA, studying film. We'd like to help her out by getting her some work on our film since her mother was so good to us.

**Santos:** Absolutely not. We don't budget for extra people being added.

**Danny:** We thought you would say that, but you can always use an extra set of hands around here I'll bet. What if her pay came out of ours? No extra budget, but another person here to help and maybe appear as an extra in the crowd scenes, if you need her?

**Santos:** Now you are talking my language. Sure. Her job is my assistant. Tell my assistant, she's hired. Then tell her to get me some coffee. We probably can use her as an extra in the film, as well. Good job, guys.

Rex and Danny go over and tell Stella she's been hired. She's elated to work with the legendary director even if her primary role is getting coffee and running errands for Santos. The entire cast and crew gathers around and gets ready for the first shots to take place. Santos gets Rex on his mark and then calls on his walkie-talkie to Jack for Gina. A golf cart comes up the hill, carrying Gina, a.k.a. Kendall Beckinsail, up to the set.

In their first meeting, Rex's attention had wandered elsewhere, but now that Gina was here, all ready to go for the movie, he looked directly at her face. She was stunning. By far the greatest beauty he had ever seen in person. She even exceeded Jennifer Lawrence, though, in her defense, he hadn't seen Jennifer on her best day.

This first shot was simple. Rex and Gina are on a miniature golf course on their first date. It's a flashback scene where Gina's character remembers the first time they kiss. Kendall Beckinsail is lining up a putt when Captain Donovan stops her. He then tells her, "If you miss that putt, you have to kiss me." When Kendall Beckinsail asks, "What if I make it?" Captain then responds, "Then I have to kiss you."

They then both drop their golf clubs and start passionately kissing under a waterfall on the course until an employee comes by and tells them the water is just recycled and never cleaned.

Santos Ramirez lines up everything. Kenny "The Intern" holds up a card that says "Scene 1 – Take 1" and then Ramirez stands back and yells, "Action!"

**Captain:** Wait. Don't take the putt yet.

**Kendall:** Why?

**Captain:** If you miss the putt, you have to kiss me.

**Kendall:** What if I make it?

**Captain:** Then I have to kiss you.

Kendall and Captain both launch their clubs and embrace in a passionate kiss under the waterfall of hole #7 on the set's miniature golf course.

In Rex's mind, as he prepared for his film debut, a movie kiss would be like kissing your aunt. Something you did because you had to, not because you wanted to. As soon as he went in with Gina, he knew this was different. He felt this attraction to her, something more than simply because she was hot. This wasn't in any way like kissing an aunt. She was like true girlfriend material and the hottest woman he had ever seen. In his mind, the fireworks were going off like in the old 1970s TV shows as they kissed. Plus, Gina Dash wasn't holding back. She was going full on tongue!

Holla!

The employee came in and stopped them. Ramirez yelled, "Cut!" and that was it. The scene was over. Ramirez said he got the shot, and they were ready to move on.

No second take here. Rex now saw the downside of working with a one-take director.

The rest of the morning was spent setting up shots and filming. There were no set breaks for the entire cast and crew. The only downtime anyone had was time off of individual jobs while others were completing their work. Santos Ramirez had a strict rule; there were to be no more than three takes of any given shot. Most were done in a single take. Others, he would give two shots. He only would take three if really needed and no matter what he got on the third shot, it was going to be the final take. "Life isn't perfect," he would say.

Morning filming wrapped up at 11:45 a.m. and everyone headed over to "The Cantina," a covered outdoor dining room on the property. Even with the lowered expectations of imagining what a Santos Ramirez craft services lunch might be like, Rex and Danny were disappointed. It looked more like a grade school cafeteria line than what they thought would be offered on a professional film set.

There were no separate meals for cast and crew. No special dishes were cooked to order for those with special requests. Basically, it was a chow line with a guy in a white coat with the name "Hamburger" in script on it, dishing out the food. Everyone then sat together communally on picnic tables.

Rex noticed right away the selection for the day, chicken fajitas, looked terrible. Unfortunately, they tasted worse. As soon as the line died down, Rex approached Hamburger to give him a suggestion.

**Rex:** Hey, Hamburger, I've got something for you which will be easy to make and really can set a higher standard for your food offerings, in particular, dishes like chicken fajitas.

**Hamburger:** What's that?

**Rex:** It's called chili water. It's an easy-to-make traditional Hawaiian condiment you find on tables and refrigerators everywhere on the Islands, in particular on Kaua'i, where I am from.

**Hamburger:** How do you make it?

Rex pulled out a tattered piece of paper from his wallet in his mother's writing and handed it to Hamburger:

*Tutu's Chili Water Recipe*
*2 Hawaiian peppers, stemmed, halved and seeded*
*½ Clove of garlic, minced*
*2 Teaspoons of peeled/minced ginger*
*1 Teaspoon of salt*

*1 Teaspoon zest of lemon*
*2 Cups of water*
*1 Tablespoon of vinegar*

*Pour all ingredients other than water into a container. Boil water and add it to the bottle while still hot. Stir.*

*When cool, seal and store in refrigerator.*

**Rex:** It's literally that simple. Over time, the taste only gets better by the way.

**Hamburger:** I could make this for tomorrow. We are having chicken sandwiches tomorrow.

**Rex:** You sure could. You will be amazed how this changes people's reaction to your food.

**Hamburger:** I've got everything I need here already. Other than the Hawaiian peppers. I'll just substitute some birdseye peppers I've got in the kitchen.

**Rex:** No, you can't do that. It has to be Hawaiian peppers. Just make a copy of this recipe, and I will have my brother overnight some Hawaiian peppers. We have plenty. He can do the early delivery so you will have them in plenty of time for lunch.

**Hamburger:** That sounds great Rex. I'll give it a try.

By the time Rex was done talking to Hamburger, people had started filing out of The Cantina. He noticed Gina sitting alone so he went over and sat by her.

**Rex:** Hey, Gina, can I join you?

**Gina:** Sexy Rexie… absolutely!

**Rex:** That was some hello, make that hellos we had today, huh? Our first introduction, then our first scene together?

**Gina:** Agreed. Hey, we're stuck here for two weeks, we should hang out. I think Santos has us filming late tonight, but tomorrow he's got scenes scheduled for late in the day which neither of us are in. We should go off campus for dinner. You can help me with some character development. I was born in Hawai'i but moved away at a pretty young age. Perhaps you can assist with the back story which can only help in me getting to know Kendall Beckinsail even better.

**Rex:** I'd like that.

With that, Jack walked in and announced, "Five minutes, everyone."

**Rex:** I need to go check-in with Rochelle to see about my next outfit. I'll see you back on the set.

**Gina:** Sounds good.

Before heading out, he grabbed Danny and had him walk with him. Rex was giddy.

**Rex:** You are not going to believe this, man, I think Gina Dash just asked me out on a date.

**Danny:** No way?

**Rex:** I'm telling you, bro. We have a free night tomorrow night. She wanted to know if I could go to dinner to (making air quotes) "Tell her about Hawai'i."

**Danny:** Oh, she's good.

**Rex:** Oh my god, man, I can't believe it. We've been so busy, I forgot to tell you: I saw Gina Dash's traffic stoppers this morning.

**Danny:** What?

**Rex:** I'm not even kidding. My first experience with accidental nudity, and I go right to the head of the class.

**Danny:** You are kidding me? How did this happen?

**Rex:** It was all by chance. Just like you said it would be. Jack told me to go to the trailer on the left. I got confused if he meant my left or his… boom, I go in the wrong trailer and there she was, no shirt on.

**Danny:** Tomorrow morning, I'm walking right in her trailer acting like I am looking for you.

**Rex:** Whoa, whoa, whoa! You said no crimes occur in accidental nudity. It's all very natural and organic. It must happen by chance. This sounds stalker-ish and rather freaky if you ask me.

**Danny:** How can I go on living knowing you've seen Gina Dash nude, and I haven't?

**Rex:** Hey, man, you are talking about someone who just very well might be my girlfriend.

**Danny:** Okay, all right, I get it. Only because I'm going to strictly adhere to the man code will I back off of this. I'm not going to pursue some accidental nudity with my buddy's girlfriend. If this falls apart, I'm back on the accidental pop-in train.

**Rex:** You know you are breaking the very parameters and rules you set.

**Danny:** Hey, if it wasn't for the girlfriend thing, this would be like times of war. All rules get tossed out the window. I'm backing off, though. This is your (now Danny is doing air quotes) "Girlfriend."

**Rex:** I appreciate that.

**Danny:** One concession… you have to tell me, how were they.

**Rex:** Oh, spectacular. These should be inventoried by the *New England Journal of Medicine* as the benchmark of how breasts should look.

**Danny:** I hate you. I actually do.

The next day, filming continued at the same frantic pace. One or two takes and then on to the next shot. Danny noticed every time there was down time, as the crew worked on a new set, Rex and Gina paired off, talking. Gina was sitting a little close and stared a little too much into Rex's eyes for this to just be a matter of a couple of associates talking shop.

Danny finally got a chance to talk to him as they broke for lunch.

**Danny:** Wow, this relationship with Gina is like on fast forward. She's already got the goo-goo eyes for you.

**Rex:** Well, Danny, the history of cinema is loaded with stories of co-stars falling in love. From cinema legends like Bogart and Bacall or Burton and Taylor to newer examples like Garner and Affleck or Patel and Pinto.

**Danny:** Patel and Pinto?

**Rex:** You know, the stars of *Slumdog Millionaire*.

**Danny:** I mean you're losing it. You are now comparing yourself to stars from the golden age of Hollywood? It reminds me of the Seinfeld episode where George was comparing himself to Ted Danson, pointing out how pompous he was, and he asked Jerry, 'Who's he?' and Jerry replied, 'He's somebody.' George followed up with, 'What about me?' and Jerry replied, 'You're nobody.' George then countered, 'Why him and not me?' and Jerry zinged him with, 'He's good. You're not.' George then retorted, 'I'm better than him,' and Jerry shut him down with, 'You're worse. Much, much worse.'

Gina Dash is a little smitten with you at the moment, that is going to cool the minute she leaves this ranch, compound, jail, whatever you want to call it.

**Rex:** Why can't you just let me be happy here?

**Danny:** I am, but I'm thinking you are setting yourself up for failure. Gina Dash is incredible. She's beautiful, successful and she has a sense of humor. You are Fallbrook, California hot for this woman. Once she assimilates back into society, she's going to end up dating a contemporary, not a laid-off parks and recreation worker.

**Rex:** You may be right but isn't having dated the likes of a Gina Dash even better than never having dated her at all?

**Danny:** In theory, I agree. Unfortunately, I'm not thinking this theory is going to pan out as you figure it is going to. I'm guessing you get tangled up in her web and by the end of this you aren't thinking how great it was to have known love and lost it rather than never having found her love at all.

**Rex:** We will see.

**Danny:** Fair enough, let's get lunch.

As they approached The Cantina, there was a totally different vibe than there had been the day before. It was palpable. Rather than everyone quietly sitting around eating their lunch, there was a buzz. People were talking about how great the food was despite the fact the chicken was basically a repackaged approach to what the chicken they had in the fajitas yesterday.

As soon as they got close to Hamburger, it became clear what was going on.

**Hamburger:** Rex, my man, this chili water is incredible. Your brother came through with the peppers, and it's so good it's unbelievable.

**Rex:** I told you.

**Hamburger:** I've got people coming up for seconds today. I can't say that happens very often around here.

**Rex:** Hey, a whole state can't be wrong. Your Hawaiian connection set you up here.

**Hamburger:** My mind is racing about what we can make next where your chili water can really enhance the flavors. This is why I got into being a chef, not dishing out slop everyone is turning their nose up at.

**Rex:** Hey, I'm glad to help out. Now set me up with a chicken sandwich… extra chili water, please!

The guys finished out their lunch (with Danny sitting between Rex and Gina) and then got back to filming. Right as Santos planned, of course, Gina and Rex finished up early and then headed off to their trailers to get ready for their night out.

Rex and Gina proceeded to a nearby restaurant where they were able to get a corner booth and really enjoy some privacy as they talked. Rex decided to heed the advice of Danny and to try to determine if Gina truly liked him for himself. He felt he had one shot at winning Gina over so he was determined to go all out on this date. There would be no guarded conversations or games. He wanted to walk away with Gina really knowing who he was… and if she was going to like Rex, she would be actually be falling for Rex Palakiko, the person… not the writer and actor on the set of **Kapu Powers**.

With his resolve to be completely himself, when Gina asked about pets, he was more than happy to share why he doesn't like cats or dogs.

**Rex:** Since I was a child I've known I've been highly allergic to cats and dogs. Knowing this was the case, we never had pets in our house when I was growing up.

**Gina:** Really? That's pretty sad.

**Rex:** It's sad unless you have allergies like I do. Like this one time, I was dating this woman with a cat. Now I know I better. I couldn't be anywhere near that thing. It meant I really shouldn't be in her house, even if the cat wasn't around. If I was sitting in a room a cat had been in, I'm going to start with my eyes itching, sneezing and my throat getting scratchy. That being said, we had been dating a short time and really hadn't gotten too personal yet, if you know what I mean.

**Gina:** I think I can figure that one out.

**Rex:** As I'm dropping her off, she invites me in. I'm sitting there, in her driveway with a little angel and devil on each shoulder telling me why I should and shouldn't go into her house. Well, you know who wins that battle.

**Gina (shrugging):** Of course.

**Rex:** So we go in and I end up spending the night. I wake up the next morning with that cat lying on my chest. My eyes were swollen, one all the way closed, and the other a tiny little slit making it almost impossible to see. In my mind, it's really not a big deal, but the chick was freaking out as she's looking at me. Sure, I looked like Freddy Krueger, but the only way to get better is to go to the doctor and get prescribed a steroid or histamine or something. I'm not exactly sure what helps... hence the need for a doctor.

Well, my doctor isn't the type where you can just call in and talk to his receptionist, relay your symptoms and then get a call-in prescription. You have to set-up an appointment. His office is always busy, so they either want to put you on standby in case someone cancels, or set it for like 6 weeks out. By that time, what's the point? I'd be over it, anyway.

If I was retired, or perhaps independently wealthy where I didn't have to work, I would stick it out and let it get better on its own. I work in an office, though, and I don't want to be some sort of freak show. I mean who has the time or desire to answer questions about a condition like this every five minutes? I can just see myself blurting out 'I am human!' the entire day so I realized I needed to get this taken care of sooner than later.

The local pharmacy had just started with the clinics in their stores where there is a person who can check you out right on site and write a prescription you can get filled right there. I decided I would go ahead and utilize the in-pharmacy clinic to get this situation resolved.

I get up to the pharmacy and head back to the "clinic" section. 'Pretty straightforward so far,' I think to myself. I sign in and proceed in to the examining room. The lady comes in to examine me and I am impressed. She's really young and good looking. She has me sit on the little examination chair with the paper on it. I step up onto the built in stair and sit down with my hands resting on my knees. She takes one look at my face and says, "Ah, allergic reaction. Do you know what caused it?"

"Yep, I get this occasionally. It's from a cat my girlfriend owns," I state confidently. I am thinking, examination over… I'm heading home with my prescription. With this, she startles me as she jumps up on the built in step to get a closer look. She was a small woman so she needed the extra height to be on even keel with me. She starts to examine my eyes, but that was the least of my worries at that point.

When she did her "jump move," her crotch came down square on the back of my hand which was resting on the back of my knee at the time. Through her Lycra-Spandex issued pharmacy pants, I can actually feel far more than I am comfortable with.

Oh so slightly, I try to move my hand out. Not happening. It's wedged firmly between my knee and her Margaret Thatcher. If I even try to wiggle it out, this situation is about to get really weird.

I actually start to break into a bit of a sweat. She keeps talking to me about how I came in contact with the cat. Of course, I don't want to go into the whole story about the woman and spending the night so I'm stumbling through my answers. She then decides to take my blood pressure (rising quickly I am guessing).

Finally, I get my prescription and get out of there. As you can imagine, the woman I was dating felt bad about the whole incident so she dropped by my apartment to make sure I was okay that night after work. In the meantime, I've got issues beyond my swollen eyes. I'm wrought with guilt over the whole incident back at the clinic.

**Girlfriend:** How did it go?

**Rex:** Um... fine.

**Girlfriend:** Did you see the person at the clinic?

**Rex:** I did, she wasn't attractive or anything if that's what you are saying.

**Girlfriend:** What?

**Rex:** Everything is good. I'm fine. Nothing happened.

**Girlfriend:** What do you mean nothing happened. You did get examined right?

**Rex:** Yes... yes, of course. I was examined.

**Girlfriend:** You seem weird.

**Rex:** They say the medication can make you a little off.

**Grilfriend:** I'm sure it can, but it's sitting there in the bag and it's stapled shut. You haven't even opened your medication yet.

**Rex:** Exactly. I need to take it and then go rest for a while. I'll talk to you tomorrow.

Whew, it was a close one! Luckily, we broke up a week later. I really couldn't handle that cat. I tell you, though, that chick at the clinic sure stuck the landing.

10.0!

Gina Dash was in tears. She couldn't catch her breath she was laughing so hard. It appears she likes the real Rex Palakiko.

The next two weeks were filled with exciting times for Rex. He saw the characters and story he created come to life under the direction of Santos Ramirez. His relationship with Gina Dash grew stronger each day. Most surprisingly were the opportunities which began opening up for him.

Team Ramirez was apparently talking up **Kapu Powers** with their friends at various movie studios and others in the industry. Several times each day Rex was fielding calls with people who wanted to work with him. This varied from small time directors looking to cast him in acting roles, producers inquiring about other material he wrote to companies looking for product placement in future projects. Most exciting was a call he took from Quentin Tarantino's production company looking to option his next story.

Life would actually be perfect if it wasn't for one small detail: his friendship with Danny Bandera began to fracture. As Rex became closer to Gina Dash and more involved in the acting and production of the film, he began spending less-and-less time speaking to Danny who had basically been relegated to a gopher on the set.

On the last day of filming, Danny finally approached Rex.

**Danny:** Rex, I just wanted to let you know I'm heading back to Kaua'i this afternoon.

**Rex:** What? Danny, I thought we were staying in California until after the release of the movie? I thought we wanted to be part of the editing process as well as the release of the film into theaters?

**Danny:** That was we said, but things have changed. I don't even really talk to you on the set anymore.

**Rex:** I've been busy, man. We're still buds. You should stay.

**Danny:** No, it's a done deal. I've got my airline ticket and everything.

**Rex:** What are you going to do back in Kaua'i?

**Danny:** I actually don't know. I even tried calling Sam Māhoe. That was a no-go.

**Rex:** Was he a trouser pilot about it?

**Danny:** No, he was nice. He just said he's moved on. In fact, he's got two new guys who have already taken our place.

**Rex:** We've got all of these opportunities in front of us. I'm on the phone everyday making deals. What about the Quentin Tarantino film option?

**Danny:** That's all your stuff. These are deals you made. I'm just a guy hanging around and getting Stella Davis coffee. I'm like the assistant of the assistant around here.

**Rex:** All of those deals are our deals. I was going to loop you in on all of these opportunities. It's Rex and Danny all the way.

**Danny:** Nah. I'd just be some guy tagging along. You don't need me. Plus, you've got Gina.

**Rex:** So that's what this is all about?

**Danny:** No, not really. I mean her being there is going to hamper our ability to hang out.

**Rex:** So it *is* about Gina?

**Danny:** No, it's not. Really. It's just that you wrote the movie. You're starring in it. These people you are making deals with, they want to deal with you. I feel like you're starting off on the wrong foot by trying to force me in. Rex, you have a tremendous opportunity in the movie business here, you need to run with it while you can. Hey, if you hit it big time, and there's a role for me, you always know how to reach me.

**Rex:** All right, buddy. If it has to be this way, I guess it does. I'll check-in with you after we get the box office numbers.

**Danny:** Sounds good. Give me a shout out when you get back to Kaua'i. We'll go to Kintaro's.

**Rex:** You got it, brother.

After a quick man hug, Danny left, grabbed his bag from his trailer and headed to the airport.

Even with his best friend leaving, Rex wasn't going to get down. Things were simply going too well in his life to let the situation with Danny hamper him from enjoying every other aspect of his experience in making his movie.

In two weeks he will be the talk of Hollywood.

Movie box office is all about the first weekend. A picture is either going to find an audience or flounder if it trips up out of the gate in its weekend debut. This is magnified in the case of a small budget feature like Santos Ramirez produces. With big budget pictures, a movie can make back its entire budget in the first weekend and the profits come in the ensuing weeks as the new audience members find the picture based on word-of-mouth or rabid fans go for a second viewing. Each week may be bringing in less-and-less in terms of receipts, but every ticket sale represents profit in the latter weeks of a film's theatric run.

With Ramirez's films, a successful box office in the first weekend means his movie has earned its keep. Distribution could possibly expand since early release is very limited for his films. Weeks two or three could potentially be the top grossing weeks for his movies. A disastrous first weekend, though, means it's going to get pulled to make room for other small films looking to take a shot at catching the attention of the public at large.

Santos Ramirez had prepared Rex with the numbers he needs to know. Four million dollars equals his breakeven point. Over five million means *Kapu Powers* will likely receive expanded distribution in the coming weeks and six million means it's a hit which will get national notice and could significantly grow in the weeks ahead.

Conversely, anything less than three million dollars means the movie will likely get pulled immediately, and Santos will have lost money. Santos Ramirez doesn't like to lose money. Luckily, it doesn't happen very often for him. Maybe once every two or three years. Plus, he's got a really good feeling about *Kapu Powers*. For a guy who produces movies like a factory, he's pretty smitten with his first ever superhero offering.

There is no hoopla, or red carpets with the opening of a Santos Ramirez film. Actually, around the time a movie is getting ready to open, it's always a busy time for him. He's preparing to start shooting on his next movie.

*Kapu Powers* is no different in that regard. Santos is once again holed up in his compound, working with the new group of actors and cast on his next feature, a teenage romp called *Spring Break Canada*. With Gina being back on the road with the Cha-Chas, and Danny back in Kaua'i, Rex is spending opening weekend alone. Sure, he had done a little publicity leading up to the premier, but most of the promotional work Santos' team lined out for him was with bloggers, internet radio hosts and podcasters. This was all completed by the time the film was ready to debut.

The news media latches onto the Sunday night numbers to report the box office winners each week. These are based on actual tickets sold, though there is some projection used for the Sunday afternoon and evening receipts.

The barometer the studios use to measure success is very different. They use the projected weekend numbers released at noon, California time, each Saturday. While they are not the final numbers, there is a high degree of forecasting accuracy with these projections and movies are considered a hit or a miss based on the early forecasts.

At 12:03 p.m. on Saturday, Rex's phone rang. He assumed it was going to be Santos, but he didn't recognize the number. When he answered, he was surprised to hear it was a representative from a vodka company who had approached him about product placement in his next movie. The representative informed Rex they wouldn't be able to move forward with the partnership based on the box office numbers of **Kapu Powers**. When Rex inquired about what the numbers were the rep told him he didn't have access to them, but he had been instructed to pull the offer.

When the phone rang again a few minutes later Rex didn't have the excitement he had just a moment before.

**Rex:** Hello.

**Santos:** Rex, it's bad. This is a real setback for Santos Ramirez Studios.

**Rex:** How bad is it?

**Santos:** $217,000.

**Rex:** Mr. Ramirez, I'm sorry.

**Santos:** We made a great movie, Rex. Unfortunately, I don't think we connected with the audience. What am I saying? Obviously we did not connect with the audience. They don't want a low budget superhero movie. Nor do they want a superhero they've never heard of. I got trapped into these four hundred million dollar box offices for these big budget Hollywood movies thinking if I made a movie a little bit less quality, maybe I'll get a payday just a little less than the big guys get. With the buying public, it's either all or nothing with genres like superheroes.

**Rex:** Maybe it will find its audience in the secondary market. You know, DVD sales, streaming or TV.

**Santos:** Maybe, Rex. This is an epic loss, though. Probably my worst ever. If this happens again this year my whole studio could be at risk.

**Rex:** Well, I have all of the respect in the world for what you do. Thank you for taking a chance on me and I'm sorry it didn't work out for either of us.

**Santos:** Better luck to you, sir.

Phone call after phone call followed Santos' call. All bailed out on their proposed deals with Rex. He knew it was coming, but nothing hurt worse than when Quentin Tarantino's office called telling him they were opting not to exercise their option.

Rex's dreams of becoming part of Hollywood were over. That night, when Gina called him after her show in Boston, he was relieved to finally speak to someone about something other than his failed movie career. He looked forward to hearing from his girlfriend and, maybe, getting a little support and a few positive affirmations.

After a few minutes of chit-chat, Gina blindside him by saying she had heard about the movie, and she knew the timing was terrible, but she was going to need to move on. She was going to focus on her career, and herself, so she simply didn't have time for a relationship.

Factoring out the deaths of loved ones, the failure of *Kapu Powers* was the worst thing to ever happen to Rex Palakiko. Having lost all of the deals he had made based on the anticipated success of the film just felt like it was piling on. It was kicking a guy when he was down.

The Gina Dash breakup took his sadness to a whole new level. It felt like he had been stabbed in the heart and then someone poured peroxide in the wound.

Rex had no idea what he would be doing moving forward and, frankly, he didn't care. The only thing he knew for sure is he didn't want to be in California a minute longer. He got on the next flight to Kaua'i. When he got to his apartment he turned off his phone, closed the blinds and went to his bedroom.

He couldn't ever imagine a scenario where he would be leaving his house again. He didn't want to talk to a soul, watch TV or in any way be a part of society.

Rex Palakiko was in a dark place.

For the next month, Rex didn't leave his apartment.
He didn't do anything other than breathing in
followed by breathing out. He lived off of supplies
he had on hand: cans of soup, items which had
been left in his freezer for an eternity and out of
date mystery items from the fridge.

His phone also stayed turned off meaning he didn't
interact with anyone, other than a brief visit from his
mother and brother who came to his apartment to
check on him after a few weeks of no contact. Rex
assured them he was okay but refused to even
open the door. He answered their questions
through the barrier of a closed door and told them
he simply needed time.

When he heard knocking this morning, figuring it
was his family again, he wasn't going to answer.
When it turned out to be Danny, he felt like he
owed him an apology so he knew he needed to
open up.

Danny had heard the bad news about the movie
but never got an opportunity to speak to Rex. He
also knew Rex was having a really rough time. He

had tried to reach out to him unsuccessfully on multiple occasions before calling Rex's brother to make sure he was all right. Rex's brother was very concerned with the health of his older brother and encouraged Danny to stop by to see if he would open up the door for him.

Arriving at Rex's apartment, Danny knocked hard on the door and identified himself, telling Rex he knew he was inside. Despite the fact he was aware Rex was holed up for a month, he wasn't prepared for what he looked like when he appeared. Disheveled, unshaven and unshowered, Rex Palakiko opened the door for his old friend Danny Bandera.

**Danny:** Rex, you look bad. You have to take care of yourself. Your mom, your brother, me, everyone who cares about you is really worried.

**Rex:** I'm so sorry, man. So sorry for everything.

**Danny:** What do you mean?

**Rex:** I made you go to California. You lost your job. Unlike me, you loved that job. I ruined your life.

**Danny:** You didn't ruin my life. I'm a guy from St. Louis who is now living in Kaua'i. My best friend and I went on an adventure to California where we pitched a movie script to a big Hollywood studio. We ended up signing on with an independent film producer where we got our movie made. I spoke to

Bob Weir on the phone. Bob Weir! You taught me about Hawai'i and the rich culture here. Jennifer Lawrence touched my nuts! It wasn't how I always envisioned it happening, but there was actual touching nonetheless. You didn't ruin my life; you made it, my friend.

**Rex:** Are you being serious right now?

**Danny:** Absolutely. I wouldn't change a thing.

**Rex:** What about your job?

**Danny:** I owe that to you, too.

**Rex:** So Māhoe ended up giving your job back?

**Danny:** Not a chance. What did happen, though, was I went out looking for work. I stopped in at Valdosta's. You know the fine dining place?

**Rex:** In Kilauea?

**Danny:** Yeah, that's the place. I went in and spoke with the manager and asked them if they had any job openings. He asked me if I had any experience as a chef in a fine dining restaurant. I told him, 'Of course.'

**Rex:** Was that true?

**Danny:** Not exactly. I had eaten at several nice restaurants, though. So he brings me into the kitchen and tells me to prepare my signature dish as a test. This was going to be my interview. It was like being on Hell's Kitchen with Chef Gordon Ramsay. Well, I know my way around a home kitchen a little, but I don't have any real professional experience. I figure I'll go the easy route and throw together a salad. As you know, it's a really nice place so I see they've got all of this great fresh fruit available. I put together the lettuce then incorporate some of the fresh fruit. When the manager asked me what my dish was called, I said it was an old family recipe called the Treasures of Summer Salad.

**Rex:** You mean like that ditty my Anakē Marlene always used to sing?

**Danny:** Exactly!

**Rex:** Did the guy like it?

**Danny:** Are you kidding? He loved it. He told me the name put it over the top. He just really latched onto the name the Treasures of Summer for a salad. He hired me on the spot and put it on the menu right away. We are pushing two-hundred of those salads out a night on the weekends now. It's incredible. It's like all I have to do there, make those salads. It's a cake gig, man. Of course the whole time I'm making those salads I'm singing, 'Ya ta ta-ta, ya ta ta-ta, the treasures of summer.'

For the first time in a month, Rex Palakiko smiled.

**Danny:** It gets better. I work in the evenings so my days are free, so I started painting again. I'm actually selling my paintings now.

**Rex:** To tourists?

**Danny:** Actually, Ronnie Valdosta, the owner of the restaurant likes for his chefs to interact with customers out in the dining room during their down times. I started talking about my paintings as I strolled through checking on the salads. Soon the customers started buying as many of my paintings as I can paint. I'm doing so well, I'll bet I can save enough to quit and open up my Cartoos business within a year or two. It's exciting.

**Rex:** That is exciting.

**Danny:** I would have never been able to do any of this hadn't we had our whole adventure with our movie.

**Rex:** I'm so glad to hear this. It's like the weight of the world is off of my shoulders.

**Danny:** No worries, buddy, it's all good. We need to go to Kintaro's.

**Rex:** Not today. I'm going to get it together, though. I need to assimilate back into society as you once said.

**Danny:** I'm glad to hear it my friend. I will let you go.

**Rex:** All right, take care. I will talk to you soon.

Rex shut the door and smiled. The failure of the movie and the breakup with Gina seemed like a distant memory. Those things were bumps in the road of life. His friendship with Danny was real. Something he vowed to appreciate from this day forward.

His first step to assimilating back into society was plugging in his phone. No sooner had it started to power up when it started ringing. Rex didn't recognize the number but saw it was a California area code. "Could anyone still possibly be trying to back out of deals with me a month after the movie came out?" he thought to himself as he answered the phone.

**Rex:** Hello, this is Rex.

**Mitch:** Rex, no way. It's really you. Wow, I really need to talk to you. I've been trying to call you non-stop for two weeks.

**Rex:** Who is this?

**Mitch:** It's Mitch Halper.

**Rex:** I'm sorry, I don't believe I know a Mitch Halper.

**Mitch:** Yes, you do. From Santos Ramirez Studios. The chef. They call me Hamburger Halper.

**Rex:** Oh, Hamburger! Sure. What do you need? More Hawaiian peppers?

**Mitch:** No. Well, wait, actually yes; but that's not the reason I am calling. I've been trying to reach you about your recipe.

**Rex:** Yes…?!?

**Mitch:** Well, one of the extras in *Kapu Powers* has a father who is a senior vice president of product development for Buen Gusto Foods. They are a global condiment and spice company. Buen Gusto tends to focus more on specialty lines.

This extra took some of the sauce I made up based on your recipe and shared it with his dad. The father went crazy for it. He wants Buen Gusto Foods to be in the chili water business. They've been talking to me about how the hot sauce market is saturated but chili water is a line extension and could really open up grocery stores to talking to them about getting it on their shelves.

**Rex:** So you sold my family's chili water recipe?

**Mitch:** No, I haven't done anything. That's why I've been trying to reach you for weeks. We are at the end of the line here. If we don't get back to Buen Gusto, their offer is going to be taken off the table.

**Rex:** So what are you saying?

**Mitch:** I'd like to partner with you on this deal. 50/50.

**Rex:** Isn't it my recipe?

**Mitch:** Didn't I land the deal? It's a 50/50 deal if I ever saw one. Don't forget, I could have made the deal without telling you, and you would have never been the wiser.

**Rex:** You are right. So what's the offer?

**Mitch:** Take a guess.

**Rex:** $20,000.

**Mitch:** No. They do all kind of studies to evaluate what the brand is worth. They literally want to go all-in with this thing. They are going to open a small factory in Hawai'i to produce it. They know they need to have the peppers from Hawai'i to make it work.

**Rex:** So, are we talking a million?

**Mitch:** How does 14.6 million sound?

**Rex:** Are you kidding me?

**Mitch:** It's true. They are offering 14.6 million dollars. That's 7.3 million dollars each. Now you know why I was trying to reach you so desperately. Get this, your disappearance actually worked to our advantage. They thought you were holding out for a better deal so they sweetened the offer. They are also willing to throw in a brand new Tesla 2.5 Roadster Sport for each of us. Those cars sell for over $100,000. Plus, there is an offer for a ten year personal services contract at $250,000 a year to run the factory in Hawai'i producing the chili water. I'm going to let you have it since you live there. I'm retired the moment we sign this agreement.

**Rex:** So, if I take the cash, taxes eat up about half of my money, correct?

**Mitch:** I am a chef and I go by the name Hamburger. Do you really want to take tax advice from me?

**Rex:** I'm just wondering about the impact of taking cash versus distributing it elsewhere. Let me think.

Several minutes pass by and Mitch can hear Rex writing and shuffling papers. Finally he decides to check-in with him.

**Mitch:** Rex, you aren't trying to get cute here are you? They have made a fair offer. I am worried if you counter they are going to reject it and move on.

**Rex:** Yeah, I think I need to reject the offer as it stands now.

**Mitch:** What? You are crazy. I will make this deal without you. We can fight it out in court down the road.

**Rex:** Easy, Hamburger. I'm not changing the money, I just want to distribute it a little differently. Do you have a piece of paper and a pen?

**Mitch:** Yes.

**Rex:** Okay, write this down. You get your 7.3 million. You can do with your money whatever you please. For my 7.3 million, please allocate it the following manner:

-$2,000,000 goes to me. After taxes, I should have about a mil left, which is enough for me to retire with a very comfortable life on the beach. That money will be going into my bank account.

-Give $2,000,000 to Danny Bandera. Additionally, take the $300,000 and open a business account in the name Cartoos at First Hawaiian Bank in Kaua'i. Use some of the funds to incorporate the name Cartoos as a car tattooing business. Also, secure the shutdown oil change business on Kaana Street near the Kaua'i Police Department in Līhu'e. Danny wants to open his business there.

-Give $1,000,000 dollars to Santos Ramirez to fund the making of the movie *The Legend of Bear Island*, if he is willing to let it be directed by Stella Davis.

-Give $100,000 to Kiki Davis to get her out of debt for her daughter's college education and to go on a nice family vacation with her family.

-Give $25,000 for Sam Māhoe. Tell him thanks for everything.

-Give Cas Schwabe of Kilauea $500,000 in cash and offer her the $250,000 a year personal services contract. Let Bien Gusto Foods know the plant they want to build in Hawai'i needs to be in Kaua'i and Cas also needs some space to run her Akamai Juice business out of the same factory, with no cost to rent the space for her.

-Finally, give the Tesla to Bob Weir.

**Mitch:** Bob Weir of the Grateful Dead?

**Rex:** Yes, that Bob Weir.

**Mitch:** You still have like $1,400,000 unaccounted for?

**Rex:** Take $500,000 and offer to buy the Līhue Brewing Company.

**Mitch:** That seems to be a little short to buy Līhue Brewing. I think they are a fairly good size company. They even sell their beer in California. Have you tried their Coconut Stout? It's made with toasted coconut. It's so good.

**Rex:** Yes, I am vaguely familiar with their Coconut Stout. I didn't mean I want to buy the entire company. I don't need the hassles of running a business. Like you, I'm retired before the ink is dry on the contract. I just want a piece of it. Make them an offer of $500,000 for 1%. They have to go for that. If you can make that happen, I then realize the dream of owning a beer brand I love. Each beer will be like paying myself.

The rest of the cash will be going to me, too. I'm not saving a penny of that money, though. I'm going to buy a new house for my Mom and a house for my brother. The rest I am going to blow of a huge family trip. The entire extended ohana!

**Mitch:** All right. I think everything you have stated is reasonable. Give me a little time to coordinate all of this. I'll be in touch soon.

Late in the afternoon the next day, Mitch Halper called Rex to let him know Buen Gusto Foods had accepted everything in his offer. They would be building a factory in Kaua'i and Cas Schwabe had agreed to run it for them. They had secured the business name of Cartoos for Danny as well as the shuttered oil change location. Santos Ramirez had agreed to make **The Legend of Bear Island** with Stella Davis making her feature film debut as a director. Bob Weir was elated to get the Tesla and the Davis family along with Sam Māhoe were thrilled to get their cash gifts.

The only stumbling block was Garrett Kama, the owner of Līhue Brewing Company had rejected Rex's offer and countered with a half-percent ownership stake for $500,000 with no voting rights. Rex gladly accepted the counter offer and the deal was complete.

**Mitch:** That's it my friend, with your acceptance of the Līhue Brewing Company offer, the deal is complete. I guess you are officially retired.

**Rex:** I'm going to celebrate tonight.

**Mitch:** What are you going to do?

**Rex:** I'm going to go out and buy 100 Līhue Brewing Company Coconut Stouts. I'm going to store 99 of 'em in the fridge, but I'll pop open that 100th one, pour out half of it down the drain and then drink the rest. You know why?

**Mitch:** No, why?

**Rex:** Because that's my percent of the company. It's my half-percent. I'm drinking my ownership stake in the Līhue Brewing Company, tonight.

As Rex sat and enjoyed a half-a-beer later that night, he thought about the difference in the lives he had made of everyone he cared about with the sale of the chili water recipe. Just twenty four hours before he couldn't think of a reason to live. Now he couldn't imagine himself being any happier.

His grin was bigger than a crocodile at a wildebeest convention as he finished off "his" Coconut Stout.

## Līhu'e, Kaua'i
## One Year Later

Over the course of the next twelve months, Danny and Rex mostly lost touch. Not because they had any sort of rift, they were both extremely busy. Danny's Cartoos business was an instant hit. Cars were lining up around the block as owners wanted to get an auto version of a tattoo.

Not even two months into running his new company, an investor approached Danny about franchising the business. A few months later their first franchise in Los Angeles opened. Others followed in Miami, Dallas, St. Louis and San Diego. Within five years, Danny expects to have over 100 franchise locations spread out across the United States.

Rex's retirement didn't last long. He enjoyed several months of down time after taking his family on an epic vacation but he soon grew restless. With plenty of spare time, he started working on a new project. He ended up using some of the skills he learned from Santos Rameriz to make a documentary entitled, **Foodbank Kaua'i**, the story of the plight of the hungry on the Island of Kaua'i. The movie focuses on families visiting a foodbank just a short drive away from where thousands of tourists enjoy world class beaches, luaus and the beauty of Hawai'i. Rex had been so immersed in making his film, he hadn't had a whole lot of time to reach out to his old buddy Danny. With the shooting wrapped and the film edited, it seemed like a good time to check-in on Danny prior to hitting the independent film circuit. Plus, he had never gotten the cartoo of his father's police badge on the back of his Jeep.

As Rex pulled in, Danny was elated to see him.

**Danny:** Rex, hey, buddy! Great to see you.

**Rex:** It has been too long!

**Danny:** You are a millionaire. Still driving this old beater?

**Rex:** Money doesn't change me. Hey, I want to get my Dad's badge on the back of the Jeep. Here's a photo.

**Danny:** Perfect. I can do this right now.

As Danny worked up the badge layout and started working, he and Rex continued talking.

**Rex:** Did you see *The Legend of Bear Island* is up for Best Picture at this year's Oscars and Stella Davis is up for Best Director?

**Danny:** I know, can you believe it?

**Rex:** They say the Best Picture is a lock. Hollywood loves Santos Ramirez, and it's a chance to finally recognize his contributions to the industry. Stella is far and away the favorite in the Best Director category as well. It's unbelievable.

**Danny:** I guess Santos is over losing all of that money on *Kapu Powers*.

**Rex:** He's made millions off of *The Legend of Bear Island* already. The Oscar nod should add even more. Plus, I heard *Kapu Powers* is pretty strong for him on DVD. I saw he added it to his "Hidden Gem" series. Everyone once in a while someone will recognize me from the movie in the most random places.

**Danny:** Really? That's cool. What about your movie, *Foodbank Kaua'i*, how's it going?

**Rex:** Great. People really connect with the stories of the families which are featured. It's an important piece. I have great hope for the film. Even if it doesn't make a dime, I'm good with it. This was a story that needed to be told. I'm just very proud of it.

**Danny:** You should be. I saw the rough cut you sent. Powerful stuff. Hey, how's owning the beer company going?

**Rex:** My one-half of one percent? Great. Garrett Kama, the owner, he's an awesome guy. Every once in a while he throws me a bone and lets me take a shift toasting coconut.

**Danny:** You want to do that?

**Rex:** Absolutely! I don't leave the work to the people. I'm a hands-on owner. How about you and this place?

**Danny:** Man, I'll never be able to thank you enough for this. It's a dream come true.

**Rex:** I'm so glad for you.

**Danny:** I might owe you some money for something else. Did you know Valdosta's pays me a royalty on each Treasures of Summer Salad sold now that I've left the company? I'm serious, I get a check every month.

**Rex:** Ha! That's awesome. It's your money, though. Anything else you are working on?

**Danny:** Well, I have this one little thing you might be interested…

**Rex:** Really, what?

**Danny:** Look outside in the back.

Rex peaks out the window and sees a large customized van, painted with various "cartoos" and the phrase, "Cartoos Tailgating Headquarters."

**Rex:** Automatic, brah! That ride is sweet.

**Danny:** It looks great, but that's not the half of it. I'm in the process of getting one of these rides at every franchise location. They are designed to be parked at large sporting events, concerts, fairs and public gatherings. I hired a Native Hawaiian couple from Kaua'i to lead this effort. They are in the process of training two individuals from each of our locations to appear at these events with these vans to spread the word about Native Hawaiian culture. They are versed in speaking to the differences between true Hawaiian Culture versus local.

Additionally, they will be serving traditional Hawaiian fare like poke, kalua, poi, and lau-lau. It's a means to not only promote Cartoos but to educate people about Hawai'i, its people and traditions as well in a unique way.

I want to be clear, these are not people handing out leis and women in grass skirts dancing to ukulele music, this is true Native Hawaiian culture; taught by individuals with true Hawaiian heritage.

**Rex:** This is fantastic Danny. I'm proud of you. I think you can really open some people's eyes with this type of education. Hey, have you seen Cas recently?

**Danny:** Yeah, I see her all the time. She's doing awesome. The chili water business is going great as her juice business is just exploding. What about you? Any other projects in the works?

**Rex:** I've got a dandy little project I'm working on. It's about two buddies from Hawai'i who write a movie and go on the adventure of a lifetime getting it made. I'm going to need your help with that one.

**Danny:** I'm in. This story must be told! Hey, we're done here. How does it look?

**Rex:** Oh, man, that is so cool. It gives me chicken skin. My Dad would love this.

**Danny:** Are you doing anything now? Let's go to Kintaro's.

**Rex:** I could definitely use a beer at Kintaro's. Plus, as an owner of Līhue Brewing Company, it's a fiscally responsible choice to be seen promoting my brands by consuming them.

**Danny:** All right, let's head that way.

As they arrive at Kintaro's they are pleased to have Emily greet them in the bar. "What have you guys been up to? I swear I haven't seen you two in like a year." Rex responds with, "Oh, nothing much, you know, just living our lives," as he winks and smiles at Danny.

Emily then says, "Let me guess, two Līhue Brewing Company Coconut Stouts, a Tin Foil Special and a Hanalei Roll. "You got it," responded Danny as Rex nods his head in agreement.

The guys then spend time eating and drinking, reminiscing about their foray into the movie business. The discussion had more of a feel of a business meeting than the typical "Kintaro's talk" they would usually engage in as the two caught up on what each other had been doing for the last year. It stayed that way until they began to loosen up and they started talking about Rex's month in the self-imposed solitary confinement of his apartment.

**Danny:** So what were you doing in your apartment for a month?

**Rex:** Believe it or not, it was a lot of catatonic staring.

**Danny:** TV?

**Rex:** No. I never even turned the TV on.

**Danny:** You didn't talk to anyone on the phone?

**Rex:** Nope.

**Danny:** How do you plan for this? Is there like one big shopping trip before you go down this rabbit hole?

**Rex:** No, there wasn't any planning. It just happened. I flew home from California and then basically tuned life off in my apartment.

**Danny:** What about food?

**Rex:** I ate what was on hand.

**Danny:** Like...?

**Rex:** Soup. I had some expired hot dogs in the fridge. I once ate a box of stuffing. Not prepared or anything. Just a box of stuffing, right out of the box. With my hands by the way.

**Danny:** I don't think I could have made it.

**Rex:** It was simply survival. You're telling me you never ate anything weird, just to get by?

**Danny (framing out his next response by holding his thumbs together and lifting his index fingers in a pose which resembles an NFL goalpost):** 2.69

**Rex:** What?

In life, there are just certain numbers which are tattooed on your brain. Besides common things like your address, Social Security number or phone number, there are some weird ones. Things you don't have to remember but somehow do. I can always tell you Stan Musial's lifetime batting average was .331. The Gateway Arch is 630 feet high. Pi is 3.14. Another one for me is 2.69.

**Rex:** Okay. So what does it mean?

**Danny:** Well, once I had just started a healthy regime. If you know me… certainly it's a pattern. Short times of healthy eating, with vows to continue forever, mixed liberally with long stretches of chicken wings, pizza and Cheetos. This time was to be different, though. Healthy eating paired with an aggressive workout schedule.

I began combining my new healthy fare with a few laps around the subdivision each night during the week. My mapped route was approximately 2.7 miles long with lots of hills to give you a decent workout. Determined to win the battle of beating my natural disposition to being heavy, I decide to push myself to the limit. What if I only ate fruit for dinner a few nights a week? I started my first night by stopping by the grocery store on the way home from work.

Mangos, strawberries, melons, oranges, bananas. There just is a lot going on down the produce aisle. Plus, with all of these selections I would then have to prepare all of this stuff. Cleaning. Peeling. Cutting. I decide to go the easy "grab and go" route. I picked up a bag of grapes.

'Simple dinner,' I think to myself.

The checker rings them out and I see on the screen 2.69 lbs. of grapes. 'That is a lot of grapes,' I think as a 'subconscious Kat von D' begins working on tattooing that number in my inner brain somewhere. I get home where I consume the entire bag.

Man, did I mention it was a lot of grapes? I change in to my walking clothes and head out the door. As I get about halfway through lap number one, I start to feel a twinge in the stomach.

Did I get something bad for lunch I think? It couldn't be grapes, already, could it? I just ate them like twenty minutes ago. It doesn't even matter. I'm finishing this walk. I've still got about two miles in front of me and I pride myself on a rock solid constitution. I mean I have control over my bowels, they don't control me. As I get about three-fourths of the way through the first lap, I realize this twinge has progressed to a pang... and it feels like this pang is about to press the evacuation button. I start to pick up the pace as I am now onboard with the idea of taking a break halfway between my laps and stopping by the house to take care of business. No sooner than I decided to do this, I realized it was time to run.

By the time I got to the house, I'm fumbling with the keys like the unnamed teen in a slasher flick about ready to get axed. I dash to the bathroom and lift the toilet lid. As soon as I remove my pants and begin to squat towards the toilet, my bunghole is already saying, 'Clear...fire, fire, fire,' and I've got a fire hose shooting to the toilet the whole way down from my three-fourths squat to my arse hitting the seat. The closest thing I could relate this to is one of those viral videos where someone drops a Mentos in Diet Coke. Had it been perhaps a corpuscle stronger, I may have actually launched upwards off of the toilet like that rocket on the MTV promos.

What is happening to me I think? When I stand up after the firefight to survey the damage, my fears are confirmed. Even though they were consumed just like twenty minutes before, there were grape skins in the shrapnel. I suggest if you are going on a long walk, avoid 2.69 pounds of grapes.

**Rex (slapping the table with laughter):** Oh, man you are killing me. I've missed these kind of nights.

**Danny:** Me, too, man. We need to do this again, soon! We better get out of here, now though. I've got a busy day tomorrow, but I should be in good shape by 4:00 if you can pa'u hana tomorrow night? We've still got a lot of catching up to do.

**Rex:** Roger that! Pa'u hana beers tomorrow night. Coconut Stout! Gotta support my investment you know.

It seems like things were finally back to normal with Rex and Danny. They squared up with Emily and headed for the door just as *Meth Lab Zoso Sticker* by 7Horse was finishing up on the radio. As it faded out, a familiar tune came on...

Whhh, whhh, whhh, whhh...

Hearing the distinct whistle of *The Walker*, instinctively, both Rex and Danny raised a hand to slap the other. As the two buddies stood in the bar, each with a hand poised to slap other across the face, both men just looked at the other and broke into spontaneous laughter.

Whhh, whhh, whhh, whhh...

# THE END

# Special Thanks

To my mom, Sandy Akley, for her work as my first-line editor. Also, thanks to the following for their hand in editing: my wife Amy and my sister-in-law Lee Ann Sciuto.

Thanks to Mark Hansen for the unbelievable cover design. The guy is simply the best.

As always thanks to my daughter Cat for just being herself.

To my good friend Cas Schwabe. Thank you for being part of this project!

Thanks to artist Maxine Graham for agreeing to be in the book and helping me tell this story!

Lastly, lots of love for my father, Larry Akley. He's always with us in spirit.

*Pa'u Hana is an original story from the mind of author Steve Akley. Any similarity between individuals living or dead, fictitious or real, is strictly coincidental\*.*

**\*Blurring Fiction and Reality**

One of elements author Steve Akley likes to incorporate into his work is to include some of his friends into his stories. It's never actually them, though, more of a hybrid of their life incorporating some details of their real life, and some fictitious components as well. Steve met Cas Schwabe while working on his **Small Brand America** series. They have remained friends after the project was completed, and there were portions of her life which fit perfectly into the story of Pa'u Hana so he worked Cas into this book.

# Who is Cas Schwabe?

Owner, Akamai Juice Company
*akamaijuice.com*

**The Real Deal (True facts from Cas' life)**
In addition to running Akamai Juice, Cas has spent much of her career in the entertainment business and is a personal chef. You can find her selling juice at the Hanalei Farmers Market.

**Complete Fiction (Made up for the story)**
Even though Cas has many celebrity friends, she does not know Bob Weir and while she may be a fan of the Grateful Dead's music, she never followed the band out on tour.

*In Loving Memory of Larry Akley*
*1942 – 2012*

*Dad at Old Faithful*

*Dad's badge photo compliments of Kelly Brooks*
*(thanks sis!)*

# Love A Cat Charity – Honolulu, Hawai'i

*Steve Akley proudly supports the mission of Love A Cat Charity with a donation from the proceeds of the sale of all of his books.*

### Mission Statement

Love A Cat Charity's mission is to help end euthanasia of unwanted cats by caring for feral and abandoned felines, spaying or neutering them and, when appropriate, adopting them out. Love A Cat Charity emphasizes the use of Trap-Neuter-Return (TNR) technique to humanely control feral cat populations. Cats are humanely trapped, spayed or neutered and returned to their outdoor homes. TNR improves the cats' health and stabilizes the colony while allowing them to live out their lives outdoors. No new kittens are born and the cats no longer experience the stresses of mating and pregnancy.

*Support of Love A Cat Charity in Honolulu, HI, helps cats like this sweet kitty*
**Love A Cat Charity**
P.O. Box 11753
Honolulu, HI 96828
*loveacatcharity.org*

# About the Author

*Steve in a suit and casual with his "writing hat," Designed by artist Maxine Graham, from Cas Schwabe, his friend at Akamai Juice Company (akamaijuice.com)*

Steve Akley is a lifelong St. Louis resident. Sign up for his newsletter, read his blog or check out his latest work, on his website: *steveakley.com*. Steve also maintains an author's page on Amazon.com. Just search his name on the site. He can be reached via email: *info@steveakley.com*.

# Steve's Latest Works

Steve explores the world of bourbon with three new offerings: *Small Brand America V: Special Bourbon Edition* and two editions of *Bourbon Mixology*.

Steve's shares his favorite jazz songs in his latest series, *Coffeehouse Jazz*. Each edition is only 99¢ (the same as or cheaper than downloading a single song) and is available on Amazon.

# The Aloha Series

1  2  3  4  5

Pa'u Hana joins Steve's catalog as part of his "Aloha Series." Though the books are not related, Steve has written several pieces about Hawai'i. These include:

1. ***Small Brand America III*** – Features the stories of 25 Hawaiian-based food companies.

2. ***Leo the Coffee Drinking Cat™ Moves to Hawaii*** – Leo the Coffee Drinking Cat™ moves from St. Louis to Kona.

3. ***Leo the Coffee Drinking Cat™ Gets on TV*** – Leo, now residing in Hawai'i gets a part on a TV show shot being shot in his adopted home state.

4. ***A Killer in Kilauea*** – A murder mystery "whodunit" is so complicated the local police bring an eccentric genius to help them try to figure out who committed the crime.

5. ***Architect of Passion*** – Biography of Kaua'i-based businessman Greg Schredder who turned a dream into the Kōloa Rum Company.

# Steve's Newsletter

# SAP NEWS

(Steve's quarterly email available through his website)

**Steve Akley's**

*Commuter Series*

Traveling to/from work doesn't have to be boring. Enjoy Steve's 1 or 2 trip short stories to make your ride more enjoyable!

Short Stories in Steve Akley's Commuter Series:

## *Only $1.49 each!*

*"The entertainment on your ride into work costs less than your morning cup of coffee."*

## Be sure to check out Steve's website:

# *www.steveakley.com*